Blaze
THE K9 FILES

Dale Mayer

BLAZE: THE K9 FILES, BOOK 4
Beverly Dale Mayer
Valley Publishing Ltd.

ISBN-13: 978-1-773361-61-1
Print Edition

Books in This Series

Ethan, Book 1
Pierce, Book 2
Zane, Book 3
Blaze, Book 4
Lucas, Book 5
Parker, Book 6
Carter, Book 7
Weston, Book 8
Greyson, Book 9
Rowan, Book 10
Caleb, Book 11
Kurt, Book 12
Tucker, Book 13
Harley, Book 14
Kyron, Book 15
Jenner, Book 16
Rhys, Book 17
Landon, Book 18
Harper, Book 19
Kascius, Book 20
Declan, Book 21
Bauer, Book 22
Delta, Book 23
Conall, Book 24
Baron, Book 25
Walton, Book 26

Boxed Sets and Bundles
https://geni.us/Bundlepage

About This Book

Blaze had planned to go home to Rockfield, Kentucky, some day. He just hadn't expected it to be this soon …

Until Badger offers a reason to head in that direction. As a longtime animal-rescue volunteer, hearing about the plight of Solo, a shepherd with severe dissociative issues from her military days, Blaze knows he has to see this through.

Camilla, on her way to an event she's planning, tries to avoid hitting a dog as it runs across the road. Blaze witnesses the accident and stops to help, realizing this could be the shepherd he's looking for. Even better, Camilla is a hoot, and it's been so long since Blaze has had anything to smile about.

But memories run long and insults cut deep, and someone isn't happy about their blossoming friendship. Or maybe even several someones … How far will they go to stop it? And who will still be standing when this all ends?

Sign up to be notified of all Dale's releases here!
https://geni.us/DaleNews

J AGER WALKED INTO the boardroom to fill his cup of coffee. "Who decided the coffeemaker should be in here anyway?"

At an odd silence, he turned around to see Blaze Bingham sitting at the boardroom table, a guilty look on his face.

Jager raised an eyebrow. "The least you could do is answer," he said jokingly.

Blaze grinned at him, sorting photographs into separate stacks. "Personally, I think it's a silly place for the coffeemaker," he said, "but, when you get a cup of coffee and turn around, you see this big empty table. It does invite all kinds of things." He motioned at his own cup. "Which is why I haven't left."

"You're done for the day anyway, aren't you?" Jager asked, sitting down beside him.

Jager studied the man in front of him. Blaze had a scar across his cheek that twisted his features somewhat, but he was still a good-looking man. That scar gave him a badass look. Jager imagined the women would like it, if they ever got past the initial shock. But, then again, Blaze, it appeared, deliberately kept himself out of the loop from most of the social scenes. Jager wondered at that, but then they all had their own challenges when it came to getting back into the circle of life and relationships after recovering from injuries such as theirs.

"What are all those photos?"

Blaze just chuckled, spreading them in front of him. "Most people have pictures of babies," he said. "These are my babies. I volunteer at the local rescue center."

Jager looked down and saw dogs, more dogs and even more dogs. He smiled as he picked up one photo of a French bulldog, his grin wide and happy. "These are all at the shelter?" he questioned. "I hope not, because that would mean the shelter is incredibly full of unwanted animals."

"No," Blaze said. "They're the ones we've helped place. Rescuing animals is good for the soul."

"Do you have much in the way of dog training?" He studied Blaze's face intently. They still needed more men for the K9 files. They had three down, all successful. Jager didn't want to slow the momentum now. But every one of the assigned men had gone out, and not one of them had come back. Personally, Jager thought that made it a double success, but he wasn't so sure the commander who'd placed their trust in him and the rest of the guys would agree.

"I grew up raising them," Blaze said. "My dad is Newfie and Saint Bernard crazy. We had purebreds. My mom used to show them, and Dad raised and trained them."

"So you have some training experience?"

"Some," he said. "My dad is a wicked hand at that though."

"I'm surprised you didn't go into the K9 unit in the military then."

"I tried," Blaze said, giving him a lopsided grin. "But I failed."

At that, Jager's eyebrows shot up. "It doesn't look to me like you failed at much in life."

"Well, I'd like to think I failed at this one for the right reasons."

Jager waited.

Blaze picked up a photo, then slowly pulled it toward him, stacking them all together again. "See? Part of the reason those K9 dogs are in the military is how well suited they are for the grueling training they go through. But we're warned that we're not allowed to get too attached. We're told these dogs could move out, not become part of our group, and that we wouldn't have any say in the matter. We'd be handlers, not owners. Now, if we retired and the dog was retiring at the same time, that's a different story. But ..."

"You figured you couldn't go into it without your heart getting engaged."

"Absolutely."

"Interesting. How do you like working here?"

"To be honest," Blaze said, "it's just a stopgap measure. I was thinking about going home to my dad, maybe taking over the family business."

"Training Saint Bernards and Newfies?"

"Maybe other dogs," he said. "The old man keeps trying to tell me to come back. We lost Mom two years back, and he's lonely. There's just him and me now."

"Where's home?"

"Kentucky."

"You're here in New Mexico why?"

"Because I was still wandering my way back there," he said, this time the grin nowhere in sight. "It seems like I was doing everything I could to avoid going home. Going home triumphant after a promotion or willingly retiring from a long and illustrious career is one thing. Going home broken and not quite yourself is a completely different thing."

"How serious were the injuries?"

Blaze shrugged. "Compared to you guys? I'm probably not too bad. I have a prosthetic foot, missing a rib on the right, lost a little off the liver, and my spleen is gone."

"All survivable injuries," Jager said, knowing just how tough those recoveries would have been.

"Which is why I'm sitting here right now. I know I want to go home, but I haven't quite adjusted to going home less than I was."

"I don't think it's less," Jager said. "I think it's life. We make plans, then life takes you out, blows you up and says, 'Okay, so now what are you going to do?'"

Blaze chuckled. "Lord, isn't that the truth? It's been good for me here," he said, "to see everybody's issues, not just my own. The rehab center didn't seem real. Everybody had such major traumas that I could almost disassociate from it, believe I was doing better. It led me down a deceptive lane that said I *was* doing better, that—as long as I ignored it—I was better off than everybody around me, so I could return to a normal life. But, of course, the reality is, this *is* a normal life, but it's not the same one I left."

"You have to be adaptable," Jager said.

"You're not the first one to tell me that," Blaze said. "You see? You guys, you've all found partners. You've all got prosthetics of one kind or another, injuries that I'm sure go well beneath the skin, and yet, you've all done well for yourselves."

"I think a large part of that," Jager said in all seriousness, "is the support group we have around us. I had these guys. They're the ones who helped me pull through. And, even though I went … I'll use the word 'dark' for the sake of understanding at the moment … I walked away from everything and everyone. When it was time to come back to the light, I came back to these guys. Because I knew they understood. I knew they were where I needed to be. And I knew that, if I had any way at all to make it happen, I would stay close."

"That's because you were all in the same unit," he said. "And I understand that. I wish I had that, but I don't."

"No," Jager said, "but you have something else that many of us don't have, and I think for most of us we would almost take that over what we have. I say *almost* because the bonds between us are very, very tight. But you have a father—a father who loves you, a father who's willing to give you some training, a second chance, his time and energy. You don't know how much longer you have him around to volunteer that."

"Exactly why I'm sitting here going over these photos," Blaze said. "These are successes in the sense that these rescues came in, were rehabilitated and moved on."

Jager waited, knowing Blaze's next line was the one that really counted.

Blaze lifted his gaze, and once again that crooked smile peeked out. "I came here broken, not connected to who I really was. I feel like I'm rehabilitated, and it's time to move on."

"If you're interested," Jager said, "I have a way for you to go home that maybe won't feel like you're going home with your tail between your legs."

Blaze studied him, an eyebrow raising. "You're offering me a job back home? I don't know how that would work."

"Well, it's not so much a job as a mission from Commander Cross."

At that, Blaze sat back and said, "Wow. That's not a name I've heard very often."

"No. He requested our assistance with a program that got shut down, and, of course, typical of all government programs, the chances of it being reopened again are pretty nonexistent. He asked us to finish what the department had been working on when they lost their budget, their funding and their staff."

"Okay. I'm confused," Blaze said. He grabbed his cup of coffee and took a big sip, his gaze never leaving Jager's. "Tell me more."

"I can't guarantee that the dog," Jager said, after he explained as much as he could, "is still in Kentucky, but I do recall that one of them was last seen there."

"Not only could it not be there," Blaze warned, "it could be anywhere by now."

"Exactly. However, our intel so far has been spot-on with the last three."

"Interesting. And what am I supposed to do when I find this female?"

"Consider this a welfare check," Jager said. "Make sure she's okay, in good hands and living a decent life."

"Easy to do if she is in a good situation. But what if she's not?"

"Which is why we're even more concerned about following up on these animals as soon as we can," Jager admitted. "The first three were not in ideal situations. In each case though, they ended up in the best scenario."

"What?" Blaze asked. "The men adopted them themselves?"

Jager chuckled. "In two cases, yes. Ethan has Sentry, but he also gained three more with a fourth on the way. He is now doing training workshops and training the animals to be taken out in K9-specialized situations."

"Wow, good for him. But then Ethan was a K9 handler, wasn't he?"

"K9 handler and trainer," Jager confirmed. "Pierce, … well, he helped reunite his dog with her owner before she was shot by the authorities or the locals who all thought the dog was attacking humans for no reason."

"That's just wrong," Blaze said stoutly. "These dogs have served their country many times over. Why would anybody want to do that to them?"

"It's a tough thing to understand. But Pierce has also been elected sheriff in a community that badly needed an honest leader," he said. "The last one was Zane back in Maine. He found his dog, called Katch, literally being hunted. He caught up to the dog just as he was at a vet clinic, but, of course, Zane went back to an ex-girlfriend, and the two of them are together again, and he has adopted Katch."

"Well, I'm not going home to an ex-girlfriend," Blaze said, "so that won't work."

"You might be surprised," Jager said. "Consider this— we don't know who or what or why we're directed in certain places, but, if we leave ourselves open to what may come," he spoke with a big grin, "just look at us. We all arrived here without partners. And we're now seven married men who couldn't be happier."

"I could hope for something like that," Blaze said, stroking the scar on his cheek, "but I highly doubt that'll happen."

"We thought the same thing," Jager said with a nod. "Don't listen to that voice. That's fear talking. Fear that you'll be alone, fear that nobody can see past the scars. And it's not true. You've got seven prime examples right here in front of you. We found unbelievably wonderful women who could see so much more than what we did."

"Sure. But now you're adding a dog to the package."

Jager stood up and grinned. "Dogs are supposed to be chick magnets, remember?"

"Ah, so that's what you're doing. You're throwing me a bone, literally, to help me get a partner." Blaze shook his head. "There's got to be somebody better for this job."

"Maybe," Jager said. "In which case, we'll offer him one of the others out of the files." Then he added, "Besides, how many of them have families who train animals? How many of them have families and properties that can handle a K9 animal that just wants to come home and rest? Remember. This K9 has her own scars, and she's just looking for love too. And in this case she's a loner. Her name is Solo, and, if you can find her, she needs to be brought in from the cold."

And, with that, he walked out, leaving Blaze wondering what he'd just been signed up for.

CHAPTER 1

BLAZE DROVE HIS truck down the long stretch of Kentucky highway. He'd been consumed with Solo since he started this trip. She truly was a loner according to her very slim file. She'd been one who bonded the first time easily and less so each time she underwent a handler/trainer change.

After her last handler had walked away from the K9 division, she'd struggled to assimilate into her new situation. As luck would have it, Blaze was heading back home, and that was the dog's last known location. And then she had taken off, and no one knew what had happened since.

The adopted family had been stalwart in their own defense, saying the dog had not taken to any of them, even though they'd tried hard. Maybe because of that they hadn't devoted much time to finding her. As far as anyone knew, she was on her own.

Not a good scenario for a loner dog to become more isolated. Blaze's heart ached for Solo. Blaze understood loneliness all too well.

Blaze picked up his takeout coffee and winced. It was pretty bad. It tasted days old, but it was coffee, and he was still trying to stay awake on this trip. For whatever reason, he'd decided to not tell his father he was coming, and he'd thrown the rest of his stuff in the back of his pickup and hit the road. This was everything he owned, and wasn't that a shocker at this stage of his life?

When he was only about twenty miles away from his destination, he pulled up at the turnoff and stopped, parking the truck off to the side of the road and hopped out. He studied the area, smiling. It had been a long time, at least ten years, since he'd been here other than visits on leave.

Up ahead was a Mustang convertible on the side of the road. He frowned and walked the hundred yards to a woman looking down at a flat tire. "That looks pretty nasty." Then he waited for her reaction. To his scar.

"Of course it is," she said, still staring at the tire, blowing long strands of blond hair back up over her forehead. "Anything I do ends up bad. It could be just a simple flat. It could be that I had a spare in the trunk. It could be that I wasn't out here alone. And just imagine if I was dating a mechanic—I could call him, and he'd come and pick me up. But, of course, none of that is reality." She looked at him without one blink and said, "Sorry, I'm not normally this upset. But right now"—she motioned at the tire before returning her hand to her hip—"this is the final straw."

She didn't react. Not one iota. *How odd*. He liked her already. Plus, she felt familiar somehow … "So, what else happened to your day that made this the final straw?"

"It's not even the whole day. It's just the last fifteen minutes. I was driving along the highway, busy thinking about the bloody events I have to arrange for this upcoming weekend, when a dog shot across the highway in front of me. I swear to God, I was on a direct course to hit it. I swerved and then ran over something, managed to come to a stop here and then saw the flat tire."

"A dog?" Blaze asked, looking at her with interest.

"A shepherd something. A shepherd mixed with something, I mean. It must be one from a breeder around here that got loose."

"I do know a breeder around here," he said, curious about the dog she'd seen. What were the odds it was Solo? "But he breeds Saint Bernards and Newfies."

She looked at him briefly and then shrugged. "Sorry. I understand basically what those dogs are, but I don't really know the differences."

"The first similarity is they're both big," he said. "The differences, … well, there are quite a few but mostly color. Newfies are solid black and have massive heads. Saint Bernards also have massive heads, but they're usually white and brown."

"Newfies are the ones that look like bears, right?"

"To a certain extent, yes. And Saint Bernards are the ones you see in the comics with a little barrel under their neck for people lost up in the Alpine."

Her face lit up at that reference. "Right," she said. "I've seen a bunch of those around town."

"Are you from around here?"

"Yes," she said. "I'm an events planner. I started my own company, and why I would have done that I don't know."

"Like weddings and stuff?"

Her stare turned flat and grim as she leveled it at him. "*Events*. Not weddings. Unless under duress," she said. "Did you know the nicest, sweetest, most beautiful woman can turn into a nightmare ogre over her wedding? I planned one once for a friend. We're barely friends anymore. So, yeah. No, *not weddings*. Wedding planners specifically handle those events."

"So, what kind of events then?"

"Everything from music festivals to modeling shows to …" She raised both hands in frustration. "I guess even dog shows. But nobody said I had to understand the different breeds. I happen to like dogs, but I've just never been around them much."

"Are you scared of them?"

"Sure," she said. "I was bit by one when I was a kid. And, for some reason, I've never really had a chance to get over it. But I don't avoid them when I see them."

"You need to be around dogs more to get over that," he said.

"You sound like quite a dog lover."

"I am," he said. "I worked with rescues in New Mexico. Best day ever was when those animals were adopted into new homes."

"Well, there's a shepherd running around here that looks lost."

"Which way did it go?" he asked, studying the woods across the road.

"The opposite way you're looking."

He shot her a look and gazed over in the other direction. "The woods go on for miles of state land out there, don't they?"

"There's talk of a subdivision coming in between this road and the new highway on the other side of this wooded belt. I hope it doesn't. Part of the beauty of the place is the fact that we're still fairly quaint and small. Once more developments come in, we lose some of that prettiness."

"Depends on how well it's done," he muttered. "Did you hit it?"

"I don't think so," she said. "I didn't hear a *thump*, but I was honestly way too busy trying to keep my vehicle on the road."

He walked across the road and checked the ditch. "I don't see a dog lying anywhere around here."

"Thank God for that," she murmured. "I wouldn't have been able to approach it either."

"No, but you could have called for help."

"I did," she said. "I called the tow truck."

He laughed. "I think that's coming down the road toward us then."

She looked down the road. "Yes," she said. "I might get back to town at a decent hour."

"Are you that late?"

"I was late an hour ago," she said gloomily. "I need to get all this shit to the event. Today's Wednesday. It starts Friday at eight p.m., and I have way too much to do."

"If you want, I can give you a lift."

She looked at him and frowned.

He said, "I am from around here. I just haven't been home much in the last ten years."

Her eyes lit up. "You know what? I thought you looked familiar."

"I'm Blaze Bingham," he said. "Dex Bingham is my dad."

"And he's the trainer of the Newfies and the Saint Bernards, right?"

He nodded.

She reached out a hand and shook his enthusiastically. "I remember him. He's a sweetie."

"Yes," Blaze said. "To a certain extent. But, like all fathers and sons, we've had our outs."

"Yep, sure can relate to that. I have a mother and two older sisters. Thankfully we live on opposite sides of the country. That way we still love each other."

She gave him such an impish grin that it had him laughing. "And you are?"

"Camilla."

"Have we met before?"

"Nope. I'd remember."

Before he could ask her to elaborate on that comment, the tow truck approached. Blaze watched the big blue vehicle pull past and then back up and out hopped somebody he hadn't seen in a very long time. Blaze had a huge grin on his face as he waited to see if Slim, the driver, would recognize him.

Slim glanced at him briefly, looked over at the woman and asked, "Camilla, what are you doing now?"

"Me?" she cried in outrage. "Me? I didn't do anything. A damn dog went across the road, and I tried to avoid it, and somehow I must have run over something. Look at that. It's flat."

Blaze didn't want to tell her that it was more than flat. The rim itself was bent. That meant buying a new tire, at least.

"Well, this one'll cost you," Slim said.

"Cost me what?" she asked suspiciously.

He just rolled his eyes at her. "It's not just a flat tire this time. You need a whole new wheel."

She just stared at him, her jaw dropping. "Oh, no," she said. "That's expensive."

"Doesn't matter if it's expensive or not," Slim said, pushing his hat back off his forehead. "You got a car. You need four wheels. Right now you have three wheels. The good news is you can afford it."

"Maybe, but I have huge expenses too, and my business

is hardly lighting the world on fire," she said mutinously. "Still, if I need it, then get me a fourth one," she said matter-of-factly.

He stared down at her and said, "That's what I'm saying. You need a total replacement."

Blaze was amused at her reaction, but then he noted potentially financial stress behind it all. "Any chance of her getting a secondhand one? Or a pair rather?"

She turned and looked at him gratefully and then spun to Slim. "Right, is that possible?"

Slim scratched his forehead, but his gaze went from the tire to Blaze and then back again. "Maybe," he said, and then he stopped, and his grin started. "Well, I'll be."

"You still sound like a country bumpkin," Blaze said, reaching over to shake his old friend's hand.

"I *am* a country bumpkin." He looked Blaze up and down and said, "You're a sight for sore eyes. Man, will your dad be happy to have you back in town."

"Oh, I don't know about that. I haven't told my dad yet. It's supposed to be a surprise."

"Well, it's a good one. You know it's a good one. He's been hoping you'd come home for the last five years."

"I'm here now," Blaze said. "I was just about to offer Camilla here"—he stopped as she swung her gaze and those huge baby blue eyes back at him—"a lift into town with all her stuff."

"That'll go past your place, and then you have to return again," Slim said in that no-nonsense voice. "Might be better if I just take her."

"But I have a lot of stuff in the vehicle," she said. "Can you carry it all? And I need to be dropped off at the center."

Slim looked a little doubtful at that.

"Look. It's not a big deal," Blaze said. "I've got lots of room in my truck. Let's just get everything moved. Slim can get your vehicle hooked up and can let you know when he gets some secondhand tires and maybe rims."

She nodded. "Slim, you'll work on that, right? I really need my wheels back."

"I'll see what I got in the shop," he said, "but you shouldn't be driving on one odd tire."

"As you just pointed out, I won't be," she said in a tart voice. "I'll be driving on four."

It was all Blaze could do to hold back his snicker, but he caught Slim's eyes as he rolled them, so Blaze explained. "What Slim means is, if you can't afford to buy four new tires, you need to at least replace two, so you're two and two."

"Why would I do that?" She stared at him in outrage. "Only one is broken."

And Blaze did something he hadn't done in a very long time. He started to chuckle, and that chuckle ended up in true laughter, and, before he was done, he was bent over double—until, all of a sudden, he was being whacked on his shoulders. She'd grabbed her purse out of the front seat and was hitting him with it.

He stepped back, holding up his arm defensively, desperately trying to get his breath. "Sorry," he gasped. "That just struck me as terribly funny."

She glared at him. "You're not very nice."

"I wasn't laughing at you," he said, but Slim was grinning, waiting to see if Blaze could get out of this pickle. "But Slim here wasn't doing a great job of explaining that you shouldn't drive with one tire odd to the other three. They should be replaced in twos, even if one is still okay."

She fisted her hands on her hips and glared at him. Then she spun around to Slim and said, "And when were you going to tell me that part of it?" Her voice got darker by the minute.

"Now, Camilla, don't you start with me," Slim said. "I'll even help you and Blaze unload your car into his truck, okay?"

"I'll move my truck. Give me a sec."

With her silent nod, all three jumped into action. When the transfer was complete, Slim walked back to his tow truck and lowered his winch. "I'll get this vehicle loaded up. I'll take it back to my shop, and we'll see. But no guarantees. And, yes, Blaze is right. You should have four new tires, two at minimum. Plus a spare. I know business hasn't been going that great for you lately, so I'll do what I can, but you need to plan that into the budget coming up. Because those other tires are almost," he said, stopping for emphasis, "shot too."

She snorted and marched to Blaze's truck. Blaze figured maybe he was the better of the two bets after all. He managed to keep his chuckles to himself, but he patted Slim on the shoulder as he walked past and said, "We need to have a beer and catch up."

"Give me a shout," Slim said. "It's good to have you back in town, man." And he turned to hook up the small car.

Blaze turned on his truck and headed back into town. He mentally marked the location and then saw Mile Marker 26 up ahead.

"What are you looking at?"

"The mile marker here," he said, "so I can come back and look for that shepherd."

She stared at him, her eyes huge. "You'd do that?"

"Absolutely."

CAMILLA CHANNING LOOKED at him in surprise. "Wow, okay, I never knew anybody who would do that for an animal."

"My dad would, and, if you told Slim about it, I bet he would too."

"I've never been around animals much," she confessed, "so they're all just this big mystery. My mom would never let us have anything. From a cat to a dog to a guinea pig or to a hamster, they were all nasty and too much work."

"Should've brought spiders home for her. She would have seen a hamster as an easy pet after that."

Camilla looked at him, and then she giggled. "I happen to like spiders," she whispered.

He laughed. "I have got to tell you that you don't look like a spider person."

"Well, not those icky ones that move really quickly across the floor," she said comfortably. "But a friend of mine had tarantulas. Now they were awesome."

She knew she'd blown him away with that comment when he just muttered something under his breath and kept on driving. She snickered. "You shouldn't make judgments about people, you know? Because we all turn out to be different."

"I wasn't trying to judge you," he said, "but you're right. You're definitely different than I thought."

"Good," she said. "Never want anybody to get too complacent. Because then they pigeonhole you into a corner and don't think you can do anything." She winced at that, realizing she was probably telling him way too much about herself, but years of having people tell her that she wasn't old enough or not a big enough company or didn't have the chops to do the job had her a little abrasive on the topic. "So, what kept you away for ten years?"

"Navy," he succinctly said. "Then an accident and then surgery and then rehab, followed by trying to figure out what I wanted from life again."

She gasped in sympathy. "Oh my," she said, "that sounds terrible."

"I did return anytime I had leave and I could come though. But my parents also traveled a lot with the dog shows. We lost Mom two years ago, and I know life has been that much harder for Dad since then."

"And for you," she said gently. "Particularly if you were still healing yourself."

"Exactly," he said as if surprised at her insight. "I was planning on coming back for visit as soon as I was well enough, but she was killed in a car accident before I got to that point."

"And you didn't come for the funeral?" she asked hesitatingly. She shifted in her seat, not sure what to say. But she just couldn't imagine the pain for the entire family. "I'm sorry," she said. "I probably met your mom, but I can't remember your dad's wife, if that makes any sense."

"Makes total sense," he said. "And, if you weren't into dogs, you probably wouldn't have known my mom. She was dog crazy. She was into show dogs and grooming dogs and breeding dogs, and it just went on and on and on."

"Is your dad still doing that?"

"I think so, at least to a certain extent," he said. "I'll know more when I get home."

"And here instead you're driving me into town, when you could already be at home, reunited with your father. I'm sorry."

"The day I pass by somebody in need is the day I deserve to be pistol-whipped," he said.

She smiled. "I think you actually believe chivalry isn't dead."

"It isn't," he said, his voice strong. "Neither is honor, loyalty or morality."

"Wow, okay." Just then they arrived at the center. "Can you turn into that parking lot for me?"

Obediently he followed her directions and then backed up to the double doors. She hopped out on her cell phone, calling for her assistant to open the doors. "I owe you one," she said, followed with a heartfelt "Thank you."

Blaze hopped out, walked around, dropped the tailgate and said, "Not a problem."

CHAPTER 2

SHE WATCHED AS he unloaded her things from his truck and not just to dump her supplies outside but carried it all in and placed it exactly where she needed it. She felt awkward now. She didn't know if she should offer him money for the gas or what. But she also didn't want to insult him. "Next time you're in town," she said warmly, "let me know, and I'll buy you a coffee."

He nodded. "Only if you let me buy you a meal."

Her eyebrows shot up. "Are you asking me out on a date when you just hit town? Wow, you work fast."

"Doesn't mean it's effective though, does it?" he said with a grin. "So, is that a yes or no?" He leaned his forearms on the bed of his truck, outlined with a silver metal rim that went all the way around.

She nodded. "Sure, well, let's start with lunch."

"Lunch it is." He walked to the driver's side and looked back at her. "When? And I have no way to contact you."

"Oh," she said. She opened her purse that she'd smacked him with. "Since I hit you hard enough with these, I should give you a couple." She handed him two cards. "That's my business card."

He checked both sides and noted her business name in bold big letters, but Camilla's name was nowhere to be found on her business card. No business address was given either. *Contact Blyth* and a phone number were provided. "So why is your name not here? Most entrepreneurs are ego-driven enough to want to see their name in print."

"Not me. Plus my assistant, Blyth, has to worry with the headache of dealing with phone calls. I've got enough other stuff to do. And don't even think about calling me until after this event on Sunday night."

"What is it?"

"One of those things I said I'd never do," she said with a groan. "But, when you've got a lot of girlfriends, it gets hard to get out of it."

"So this is a Bridezilla event?"

Her gaze went round, her finger went up to her lips, and she whispered, "*Shh*. Don't ever let anybody hear you say that."

He laughed, got into the truck and, with a honk of his horn, he drove off again.

Grinning, she walked back inside to see her assistant, Blyth, shaking her head, pointing an accusatory finger at Camilla. "What? I got a flat tire. What did you expect me to do?" she asked, rushing forward.

"It's not that, but I just heard you agree to a date. When was the last time you agreed to a date?"

"Too long ago," Camilla said. "Why? Am I in trouble for that too?"

"Do you know how many men I've tried to get you to go out with? And every time you ignore me. You won't let me set you up with anybody, and I know *everybody*," Blyth said, rolling her eyes.

But considering Blyth was sporting bright purple spikes on the top of her head and tattoos all up and down her arm, Camilla hadn't convinced herself that Blyth's circle of friends would contain anyone she was interested in. "It wasn't the right time," she said, walking over to the boxes Blyth had unpacked.

"Interesting," Blyth said. "So, who is this guy?"

"He's from around here. His name is Blaze. His dad trains Newfies and Saint Bernards," she said haphazardly. "At least, I think those are the breeds."

"Oh, my goodness. He's Dex's son." She looked back out at the open doors, but the truck was gone. "Why didn't you introduce me?" she cried out.

Realizing this was important for some reason, Camilla frowned, straightened, turned to look at her assistant and said, "You just gave me heck for accepting an invitation. Now you're giving me heck because I didn't introduce you?" She shook her head. "Talk about double messages."

"Whatever," Blyth said. "His mom was a beautiful woman. It was so sad what happened to her."

"I don't remember her," Camilla said sadly. "He told me that she died in a car accident two years ago."

"She not only was into show dogs," Blyth said, "but she was a model. She's in all kinds of pictures around town. She never charged anybody, so a lot of them took advantage of that. Her only request was, if the photos could handle it, that she have a dog with her. Because that's how she wanted to be known, as the dog lady."

"Oh, wow, that's an interesting thing," Camilla said. "Now that you mention it, I think I've seen her."

"You've seen her," Blyth said reassuringly. "You've seen her lots. She's on the library billboard thing there because she was a patron. She's got a picture at the dance hall because she and her husband were crazy dancers. I can't remember all the places where her face is, but you have definitely seen her around this town."

"I'm sure I'll look for it now," Camilla promised. "But for the present, back to work. Where are we?"

Blyth pulled out her iPad and started ticking off boxes. "We've got the cutlery and the dishes. We've got the centerpieces. We've got the tablecloths. We've got the candles," she said. "We're waiting on the flowers."

"They aren't coming today though, right?"

"Nope, but we have the dress rehearsal tomorrow night, and we need the flowers for the entranceway. There is a problem, though, with the bouquets." Blyth winced as she looked up. "Right. There's always something."

Camilla looked at her assistant in horror. "You can have problems with the flowers on the altar. You can have problems with the flowers at the dress rehearsal. You cannot have problems with the flowers in the bouquets."

"I know that," Blyth said. "I've got several calls in. We're trying to see if we can get something, but Lizzie wanted that tiny pink baby's breath. And apparently the pink didn't come in, so the florist only has white."

Camilla slowly rubbed her temple, feeling a headache coming on. "I need to call her then. That won't work. We must have pink. Remember? That was the one thing Lizzie said was nonnegotiable."

"Nonnegotiable per the bride is one thing, but nonnego-tiable when we can't get it two days out is an entirely different thing," Blyth said.

"I know," Camilla groaned, staring up at the ceiling. She opened her arms as if to say, *Why?*, and then said, "Let me talk to the florist. There might be a way."

"You call her," Blyth said. "And I'll start unpacking this stuff."

Nodding her agreement, Camilla pulled out her phone and called the florist. "I know what you'll say, Camilla," Wanda said. "But there's no help for it. I can't get any pink in. I can't get it in today. I can't get it in tomorrow, and I can't get it in Sunday."

"In other words, it's not happening. Is that what you're saying?"

"Exactly."

"Spray paint?" Camilla asked.

After a bit of silence at the other end, then Wanda laughed. "Oh, my God, is it that big a deal?"

"It's not supposed to be nonnegotiable," Camilla said, "but, of course, it is. Right? It's one of those things you can't get, that, of course, I need."

"I'll take a look. I don't think I can even dye them."

"We've got to try. Obviously spray paint is not the best option."

"I'll consider it," she said. "I don't know what I'll do, but I'll find a way."

"Thank you, thank you, thank you," Camilla sang out before hanging up. She danced around to see Blyth staring at her.

"Did you just say, spray paint the baby's breath?"

"One must do what one must do."

Blyth shook her head. "That's almost sacrilegious."

"What am I supposed to do?"

"I don't even want to think about it, but you could tell the bride that she can't have it."

"I'd rather die," Camilla stated. "You know she'd kill me."

"This is why you don't do weddings."

"Which is why I didn't want to do this one," Camilla

said.

"Too bad you didn't listen, isn't it?"

BLAZE WAS STILL chuckling as he headed toward his father's place. He didn't remember Camilla growing up. He'd ask his dad about her.

Finally the turnoff came up ahead, and he turned on his flasher and made the turn. The road was rutted more than he expected, but then again Mom always bitched about the road and how it upset the dogs to get bounced all over the place. She was the one who had the grader come in once a year to clean it up. Obviously Dad hadn't.

Blaze still chuckled to himself when he pulled up in front of the huge log house. His dad's truck was there, and his heart hitched when he saw the place where his mom's SUV should have been parked. He sat here for a long moment staring at it and then pushed open the truck door and hopped out. He could hear dogs barking in the background, but then when had he not been home to the sounds of dogs barking? This had been his mom's life. It had been his dad's life. Blaze just didn't know if it was currently part of his dad's heart anymore. The loss of a loved one often changed everything.

He took the front steps two at a time and pounded on the front door and then reached for the handle and pushed it open and stepped inside. "Hello?"

A yell came from the back of the house. He walked through and stepped out onto the huge veranda that floated down the whole back of the house, and there was his dad, standing out in the yard, two dogs at his heel, a ball in his hand, idly throwing it for them.

His father turned and let out a *whoop* that had all the dogs clamoring. The two dogs at his side raced toward Blaze. He didn't know these two, which meant the old two he'd seen last were gone. His dad grabbed Blaze and hugged him tight. "Jesus Christ, you're a sight for sore eyes," he said. He stepped back, gave Blaze a hard shake and then hugged him again.

Blaze wrapped his arms around his dad and just held him close. The two men stood like that for a long time. When Blaze stepped away, his father wiped the moisture from the corner of his eye. "I'm sorry, Dad."

His father just nodded. "I'm not exactly sure what you're sorry for, but we'll shelve it for the moment. It's damn good to see you." He stepped back, looked his boy up and down, and Blaze grinned.

"It's really me."

"All in one piece?"

"What's left of me, yes. I might have lost a few pieces," he said.

His father's frown was instantaneous. "I knew about a lot of it," he said. "You were having surgery, and you were in rehab, and we talked on the phone but with your mom's accident ..." His father's voice trailed off.

"I know. I couldn't come for the funeral. I've been healthy for quite a few months now. At least I was physically, but I was struggling with that whole 'What will I do with my life?' thing, and I didn't want to come home when I didn't have any answers."

"Home is where you come when you need to figure out answers," his father said. "But I won't chastise you for that now. I'm just too damn glad to see you." He walked inside and said, "Come on. Let's put on some coffee, and we can sit outside and shoot the breeze."

Knowing his father just needed a bit of time to settle down, Blaze let Dad brew the coffee while Blaze studied the living room. It didn't look any different. Mom's throw blankets were on the back of the chairs, and her pictures were all around. He walked over to one he didn't think he'd seen before and studied it. "She was really beautiful, wasn't she?"

"She was, indeed," his father said, his voice thickening. "Inside and out. A lot of people tell me it's supposed to be time for me to get out there, try dating again," he said, "but I can't do it. She was the one and only love of my life, and I just don't think anybody else out there is someone I care to spend time with."

"I don't think you're supposed to go out looking to replace Mom," Blaze said gently. "I think you're supposed to look for companionship, hoping to find a friend, somebody you can talk to, maybe do things with."

"I haven't done that either," his father said. "The trouble is, I know I need to. It's been two years, and I've still got everything exactly the same, and I need to move on, and I need to let her go." He stopped, put down the can of coffee and looked over at Blaze. "But I just can't."

"I'm not pushing you to," Blaze said, stepping forward. "When you're ready, you'll do it. And, if you're not ready and if this makes you happy, tell everybody pushing you to shove off."

His father's face lit up with a big grin. "Damn, it's good to see you. That's exactly the attitude I've been looking for. Somebody to support me rather than telling me how it's good for me to get out there and do things."

"Hey, I've had more than my share of that too."

His father's face lost its mirth. "I can imagine," he said. "That's a hell of a scar you're sporting."

"I know. A piece of jagged metal from my accident."

"Are you looking into getting it fixed with plastic surgery?"

"No," Blaze said. "I'm waiting until people just accept this part of my face and stop looking at it. Speaking of which, I just met some ditzy female who didn't seem to even notice."

"You met somebody already?" His father looked up at him and frowned. "How?"

"Her Mustang had a flat tire on the road," he said. "Camilla somebody-or-other." He reached into his pocket and pulled out her cards. He handed one to his dad.

His dad started to chuckle. "Oh my, Camilla is a special case."

"Maybe," Blaze said. "But honestly, she seemed to be exactly who she was, and that's a bit different."

"She is something. She's full of heart, full of humor, and just sometimes I think she's from a different planet," he said, as a nice way to putting it.

"You mean, other than the fact of Mars and Venus?" Blaze said, referencing that old book about the differences of the sexes.

"Exactly," his dad said. "Camilla knows a lot of people in town. She's heavily involved and apparently doing all these events," he said, dropping her card on the counter. "And you won't hear anything bad about her. Her sisters and her mom, now, that is a different story."

"Not quite the same?"

"Those three are more after a solid match that would

move them up the food chain," he said succinctly. "Your mother never did like any of them."

"How long have they been in town?"

He shrugged. "No clue. They might have arrived just about when you were leaving."

"I certainly didn't recognize Camilla. I did see Slim though."

"Slim's a good guy," his father said. "He's taken over the family business."

"Good for him," Blaze said. "He didn't look a bit different."

"No, Slim's still pretty much Slim. And you," his dad said, turning to him. "Are you the same inside?"

"No," Blaze said easily. "Neither are you. We can't go through the things we go through and still be the same. The core of who we are is there, but every day we're a different person because we adapt and adjust to the new reality of a new day."

His father nodded and said, "Very true, very true." He poured a cup of coffee for each of them, handed one to Blaze and said, "So, you didn't tell me that you were coming. Are you staying? Are you here on a mission? Are you working? What's going on?"

His father led him outside to the big bench on the porch, and they sat down. "It's a long story," Blaze said, "but let me see if I can give you the shorter version." And he explained about Solo.

"Oh, interesting," his father said.

"And oddly enough," Blaze said, "Camilla said she ran off the road and hit whatever gave her a flat tire because she avoided a shepherd running across the highway."

"Or she just wasn't looking," his father said with a

chuckle. "But the mention of the dog is possible. I have heard about a shepherd around these parts. Any idea how long Solo might have been here?"

"About four months," Blaze said. "I was hoping you would know something about her."

"Can't say I do," he said. "I do know a lot of the dogs around here. But you know what it's like. Lots of dogs run loose here. We keep trying to fix the problem, but most of the way they get fixed is with a bullet."

"I know, but I'm hoping not to do that or to hear that has happened in this case."

"She really served our country?"

"She really did," Blaze said. "So did I. And I got rescued, and I'm starting to feel like maybe I have a purpose again, so I would like it if Solo could be rescued and could also feel like she has a bit of a purpose again too. If nothing else, she's owed a decent life for what she did for us."

"Damn," his father said. "To think a dog brought you back." He started to chuckle.

"What's so funny about that?" Blaze asked.

"I figured it was the dogs keeping you away," he said. He motioned out to the pens. "I've got twenty-two dogs right now. And I know it's not always been your thing, so I figured you were afraid of coming home and being roped into the family business."

"It's not that at all," Blaze said. "I've come to enjoy the truly finer things in life, and that means space, animals and home," he said with a smile. "But I also needed a purpose and a reason to come home that wasn't because you wanted me here. It needed to be," he said, "and I don't mean this in a bad way, but it needed to be because I wanted to come home."

His father's piercing gaze met his. "So, are you here because you want to be, or are you here for the shepherd?"

Blaze looked at him and chuckled. "Honestly, I'll say both. The last thing you need is another dog. But she's a lost one, just like I am, and, if you're willing to take me back home, maybe you'll be willing to take her too." He had no intention of letting Solo suffer any longer if he could provide a permanent solution.

"If she comes with you and that's the package deal," his father said, "it's done. You're more than welcome, both of you. But you've got to find her. You've got to track her. You've got to train her, and you've got to look after her."

The two men looked at each other and grinned. "Just like the old days," Blaze said, remembering his childhood and his request to have dogs of his own.

"That's what life's all about," his father said. "It's all about things going around and coming around."

"I'd like to think I'm home, and I'll find something here that makes me feel that way," Blaze said.

"In that case, you should probably invite Camilla out because the best way to feel at home is to have a girl."

"Advice from my dad, look at that."

"Hey, if you can avoid her mother and her sisters, Camilla is gorgeous," his father said. "She's unique, and I'm not sure that's bad. Plus, she's a good-hearted person. You could do a lot worse."

"What's with her family?"

"Remember how your mother hated Lily?"

Blaze frowned but nodded.

"That's Camilla mother."

Blaze just shrugged. "Water under the bridge, right?"

"And they moved off to California years ago."

"So, you won't be too upset that I've already asked her out for a lunch date then, right?"

His father looked at him and shook his head, slapping his thigh. "Wow, you haven't even been in town an hour, and you've already hooked the most eligible female. Way to go, way to go."

"Most eligible? How do you figure?"

"She's slim. She's pretty, and what you didn't know is she's got money. Big money. The thing about her is, you'd never know it."

CHAPTER 3

CAMILLA WORKED HER way through her to-do list, trying to keep the stress and the stomach knots at bay. She'd been through this enough times that she knew there was a system and that the system worked. She'd worked hard to make that system work. She and Blyth worked hard for the rest of that evening. Only as she was packing up with a sigh of satisfaction at how much she'd managed to get done did she suddenly freeze. "Oh, my God!"

Blyth said wearily, "Now what?"

"Oh, my God. Did you mean that his mother, the model, the one with the dogs I couldn't place was Enid?"

Blyth's face slowly broke into a huge grin. "You finally remembered?" she crowed.

"I didn't make the connection right away. You don't understand," Camilla cried woefully. "That's not a good thing. Enid and my mother hated each other. Why couldn't she have been somebody else?"

"What difference does it make?" Blyth said. "Your mother's not here anymore."

"Sure, but she has spies everywhere," Camilla said with a wave of her hand, as if Blyth's concern was nothing. "You know that."

"You have to stand up to your mother sometime," Blyth said unexpectedly.

With a dark look in Blyth's direction, Camilla turned her back and said, "I've been standing up to her since forever. It doesn't make any difference. My mother is a force unto herself, and it's rarely in a nice way."

"Yep, that's why she and Enid didn't get along. Your mom didn't see the point in having dogs, thought dog shows were useless and hated the fact Enid's face was all over town."

"Of course, because my mother prides herself on her looks and thought *she* should have her pictures all over town." Camilla shook her head. "Why me?" she muttered. She remembered many of the conversations now about how Enid shouldn't be in those photographs, shouldn't be on those posters, shouldn't be the leading face of this or that. Her mother had had a major case of jealousy against Enid, and, as Camilla thought back on it, she wondered just how deep it went. There'd never been any mention of a son or maybe a brief statement saying he'd gone into the military, whereas her mother had prided herself on her three daughters who were all, in her mind, successfully married—except for Camilla of course.

Both her sisters had married upwardly mobile wealthy males with a huge bright future ahead of them. Her sisters appeared to have the same thought about their successful marriages too, as they often looked down their snotty noses at Camilla and her quote "job."

"A little job," just one that would keep her busy but not exactly catch her a real man. An argument that had gone on for the last many years. The best day of her life—and she hated to say it—was the day her mother and sisters had all relocated out West two years ago where everything was happening. The sisters had both met and found their husbands there too. Because, of course, no eligible males were left here in Kentucky.

The fact that Camilla's grandmother had also passed on and had left a lot of her estate to Camilla had been the final driving wedge in the familial relationships. Her sisters had gotten something but not as much. Her grandmother had said Camilla's mother was the face of the family, but Camilla was the heart, and Grandma was all about helping the heart. At the time, Camilla had felt guilty and wondered if she should have shared, but her other relatives and friends had told her, "Don't." Her sisters had both drummed into Camilla how she *had* to give over her inheritance, telling her that was only appropriate, but they had all quickly disappeared when they realized she wouldn't. She still had pangs of guilt over it. But not enough to change.

Her sisters weren't terribly nice people. Camilla had not been invited to either wedding. She'd been sent lavish videos and photos though, but it was presumed she was working too hard at her little business to take the time off to go to their weddings. It had been a grave disappointment because, as much as they may not get along, she would like to think blood was thicker than water. In this case though, apparently not. Money was the only glue that held her sisters together. When Camilla hadn't forked it over—and, of course, maybe they had the right to feel angry over Grandma's split of her estate—her sisters and her mom had cut Camilla out of the family.

It's not like Camilla had decided how Grandma should divvy up her estate. And Camilla didn't cut her mother and sisters out of her family. But it took two … or, in this case, four.

Still, as she got into her Mustang, now with a brand-new

wheel on it and delivered to the door, she slowly drove back to her house, wondering if this impacted her view of Blaze. Then wondered, when he found out about Camilla's mother, would it impact his view of her? It shouldn't. They were both young adults who weren't responsible for their parents' actions or feud. But that was also easier said than done.

She pulled up to the front of her place, hit the code to open the gate and drove forward, hitting the remote button to open her garage door. She drove into the garage, closing the gate and the door behind her before she exited her car, tired and frustrated. Yet still feeling good she'd managed to get as much done as she could for this upcoming weekend. She walked inside to hear the landline phone ringing—something also handed down by her grandmother. It kept Camilla's home life separate from her business. She grabbed the phone and said, "Hello."

"I hear Enid's son came home?"

Surprise, surprise, it was her mother. "If you say so," she said cautiously. "And who told you that?"

"Never you mind," her mother said. "You stay away from him. I won't have anybody from that family associated with ours."

"So I'm part of the family now that you have a bigger, badder villain?" Getting no response, she said, "Good to know." Still wondering how her mother could possibly have known the latest gossip here so fast, Camilla took off her jacket and put on the teakettle. "I don't even know the man," she said, "and Enid's gone. Her family had nothing to do with your fight with her."

"They're all the same. Blaze is exactly the same."

"Well, he seems to care about dogs too, apparently," Camilla said, "but that's hardly the same."

"It all starts down the same path," her mother said darkly. "And I'm warning you. You stay away from him."

Camilla leaned against the counter and said, "Or what? You left here so you didn't have to deal with me, and there you are out West, trolling for yet another husband. What difference does it make to you if I date somebody here you don't approve of?"

She could hear her mother sputtering.

"I'm not trying to be insulting or disrespectful, just opening up the lines of communication," Camilla said honestly. "I am an adult. I haven't lived in your house for years. So I follow my own rules now. But I'm asking. I'm curious. Why should any feud you have with somebody—who is now dead—impact how I treat any offspring or the rest of the woman's family?"

"Because they're bad people," her mother said.

At that, Camilla burst out laughing. "Oh, my goodness, bad? Why? Because you didn't like them? How is that even a thing?"

"Don't you laugh at me," her mother commanded in that haughty tone.

But Camilla could hear the hurt in her mother's words. Camilla moderated her tone. "Look. I'm sorry, but just because you decree that I shouldn't have anything to do with him doesn't mean I'm not going to. And, if you don't mind, I've had an extremely long day. I'd like to get some rest." And she hung up the phone. Generally her mother would never let her get away with that and rarely would it end there. Camilla waited, watching the phone like a time bomb, but it didn't ring again. Surprised but happy, she made herself a cup of tea and then, after it was made, stared at it and said, "I really could use a glass of wine now."

She pulled out a bottle from the fridge she had already opened and poured herself a large glass. And then she looked at the tea and the wine, shrugged her shoulders, picked up both and carried them through to her sitting room. She set both down on the coffee table, turned on her gas fireplace, even though it was the middle of summer, and curled up in a corner of the couch.

She wanted to grab her laptop and go over some of the stuff she'd done today and take some notes so she didn't forget, but, at the same time, she was, as she'd told her mom, exhausted. She dropped her head back against the high cushions and tried to destress. "Who would have thought?" she said. "Enid's son." She shook her head. She didn't think there was any other male in this town her mother would have as much of a problem with as Blaze.

BLAZE WOKE THE next morning, feeling better and more positive about life. He'd gotten over that awkward first moment with his father. They'd hashed out and discussed other issues all last evening, going from politics to religion to his mother's funeral to Blaze's own injuries and to the fact he wouldn't let his parents be at his side in the hospital. But the end result was, when they were all talked out, both men had been basically comfortable again.

With a wave at his dad, who stood on the front deck, Blaze hopped into his truck and headed back out of town to where he'd stopped to help Camilla. He knew she was having a crazy day, today being Friday, and of course, her event was on the weekend. He didn't know weddings took an entire weekend or if it just took an entire weekend to deal with the setup and then the takedown, but he figured it wouldn't be safe to call her until Monday. But he had to admit it was one of the first things on his mind when he woke up. He pulled his truck off to the opposite side of the road from where the Mustang had been parked, got out and locked up. He grabbed his water bottle, shouldered his pack, crossed the road, backtracked about fifty feet and then headed in the direction Camilla had seen the dog running.

It was overcast but warm. All in all, it was a nice day for a good walk, and the least he could do was check out the last sighting of the dog. He had a leash, dog treats and some dog food in his pack. He didn't know what kind of condition or temperament the shepherd might be in. He just hoped he could track her down and get her home. His dad had been all for it, had even volunteered to come this morning, but Blaze had wanted to get out alone and to see what he could figure out on his own.

If he found the dog and couldn't get the dog to come to him, well, calling his dad in to help might not be a bad idea. His father's methods were a little bit harsher than Blaze would normally have used himself. His mother had been a much softer trainer. But everybody had their own methodologies, and his dad had never abused an animal yet, so it wasn't like Blaze would have a problem bringing his father in to help.

He could hear the sound of the woods crackling underneath his feet. He wanted to walk quietly, but it wasn't happening. The forest was way too full of deadfall, which was too bad because, if a fire started here, it would sweep through the area and take out so much that they'd find themselves in the middle of a huge inferno.

The trees got thicker and thicker as he went. His phone's

GPS told him where he was, and, so far, he could still see his truck. He had a rough estimate of where he was going, having looked it up on satellite imagery earlier this morning. Miles of land were around here. It belonged to the state and wasn't developed, but obviously there was talk about it happening soon.

As he walked, he called out to the dog. "Hey, girl, you hungry?" He looked around, whistled a series of dog whistles he knew from his father. But still saw no sign of her. He kept walking. After an hour, he wondered if he'd gone far enough. There was a field up ahead. He stepped through the break in the woods to see a more open area. There he found a log, sat down and drank from his bottle. He loved being out in nature. Having a spot like this to enjoy was a godsend. It was one of the reasons why he had wanted to come back home. It was a decent-size town but with a lot of countryside. Much better than a huge city with no greens at all.

As he sat here, he thought he heard a noise up ahead. He turned and looked and found a couple hikers. They took one look at him and stopped.

He raised a hand in greeting, calling out, "Good morning." He watched the relief cross their faces. It was a young couple, maybe even teenagers. They waved a hand back and kept going. He hopped to his feet and called out, "I'm searching for a lost shepherd. Have you seen her?"

They talked for a moment, then called back, "Not today. We did a few days ago though, when we were here."

"Where did you see her?"

The man pointed in the direction they'd come. "But we haven't seen her this morning."

"Okay," Blaze said. "I'll head off in that direction and take a look."

The couple kept going. As they were about out of ear-shot, the man turned back and said, "Is she dangerous?"

"I don't think so," Blaze said. "But I know she's lost, and she needs a home and maybe medical attention."

The man nodded, and they kept walking.

Blaze picked up his bag and decided to follow their trail back to where they had come from. He figured they had approached this wooded area from a different street than Blaze did, and, if he followed their tracks back, he could walk the road all the way down again. And that was what he did. Unfortunately he detected no sign of the shepherd. He stood on the other side of the street and wandered around the area. There were a couple houses. He knocked on both front doors and asked if anybody had seen the shepherd. One man had; the other person hadn't. But the man who had seen her didn't have a clue where she came from. He said he saw her just walking down the street. So now Blaze had to figure out if his only way to get a hold of her was to stay in this area.

He walked back to his vehicle, tired but feeling physical-ly better after the hefty walk. He grabbed his brown bag lunch and ate his sandwich as he kept an eye out for Solo crossing the road. Finishing off his lunch with some water, he took a thirty-minute power nap. Waking up refreshed, he then decided, since the shepherd had come from the other side of the road, crossing in front of Camilla's path, there was a good chance she could be over there too. He headed into that area, figuring he'd take a quick look.

He was only in the trees about one hundred yards when he heard a sound. He froze when he saw maybe a coyote, maybe a dog, off to the far right, about another one hundred yards deeper into the forest. He took a few stealthier steps, only it was impossible to walk quietly. The leaves crackled from the severe drought, and so much underbrush was here that every step he took made noise. He studied the undergrowth, looking for the animal. It was well-hidden; Blaze's only awareness of it was the flicker of its ears.

Blaze crouched down ever-so-slightly and called out, "I'm here. It's okay."

Slowly he lowered the pack off his back and brought out the bag of dog treats. He shook the bag gently and said, "Come on, girl. Come and take a look." He remembered how the navy's K9 trainers would have called her by her name. Same thing his parents would have done too, to strengthen the connection between the dog and the human. "Hey, Solo. Come on, girl. Come say hi."

He waited a long ten minutes, but whatever was here wasn't coming forward. Finally he put the treats back in his backpack and said, "I'll be back. I promise." He pulled out the dog food and made a spot on the ground, knowing the dog's senses would easily pick it up. He dumped out a bunch. "I'll come back later this afternoon," he said, and he slowly backed away. He didn't know how long she had gone without human contact.

He waited at the side of the road, wondering if he'd see enough to confirm it was Solo, but then realized the dog would wait for him to leave the area before she went for the food. Right now, the most important thing was that she eat and stay fit, so he climbed into his truck and drove down the road a bit. There were just miles and miles of nothing up ahead. He finally turned around when the shoulder was wide enough that he could do a U-turn with his truck and pulled back up to the same place. He stopped, hopped out and followed the same path he'd taken the first time deeper into the woods.

He stopped when he got to where he'd put the dog food and smiled. "Well, at least you ate," he said. "How about a bit more?"

Still, he noted no sign of the dog, and he couldn't hear anything move, but he carefully shook the dog food bag again and then poured out some more food. Happy he was getting food into her, he hopped back into the truck and headed into town. There he went to the feed store and picked up more dog food. As he walked out, he caught sight of Slim.

"Slim," he called out. "How did you make out with Camilla's car?"

"I found one tire," he said, "and only one. But we've got her back on the road, and I'll keep an eye out for a good set of used ones. The sooner, the better, I know," he said with the shy smile, "but she needs something now."

Blaze nodded. "Sometimes we must do what we must do. It doesn't really matter if we like it or not."

"Exactly," Slim said. He looked at the dog food and said, "That won't go very far at your dad's place."

Blaze chuckled. "No, I'm after a shepherd that's been lost in this area. Have you seen her?"

"I think everybody has," Slim said. "It's almost always seen in the area where we found Camilla stranded."

"That's why she says she ran off the road," Blaze said. "She saw the shepherd and tried to avoid her."

"Yeah, done that a time or two myself," Slim said.

"Have you seen her anywhere else other than that stretch of town?"

Slim shook his head. "Nope. Now, old Freddie there, he lives probably closest to that area. You might ask him.

Although he doesn't think much of dogs, as you know."

Blaze nodded. "Then it's probably better I don't ask him. He's likely to go looking for the shepherd and pop her one."

"If you bring him a bottle, he might let you know when he sees the shepherd and not kill her, but you can't be sure about that."

Blaze nodded, pondering it. "You got time for coffee?"

"No, sorry," he said. "I've got to go out and help my mom. She's having trouble with her Jeep."

"Okay, good enough. I'll see you later then." Blaze headed to the coffee shop himself, wanting that midafternoon hit of caffeine. He looked around at the storefronts, trying to refamiliarize himself with what felt natural and normal and what felt different and was likely new to town. That baby store he thought was new. Beside it was a computer gaming store. He thought that was new too.

He went on to the coffee shop. Although it was still in the same location, it had a new name. Now it was the Hungry Hound. He walked in and didn't recognize the owner and the people working here either. He pulled out a chair at the table nearest the big window, sat down and, as soon as the waitress arrived, ordered himself a coffee. Somebody else came in behind him and ordered coffee and a cinnamon bun. When the cinnamon bun was delivered, Blaze's eyebrows rose up high. He called out to the waitress and said, "That looks wonderful. Could I get one too, please?"

She smiled and said, "Sure." She disappeared into the back.

He sat at the window, watching the world go by, wondering what had brought him back here at this time. It was good to be back. It felt right to be back. He just wondered at the odd sense of not having come back all this time. There were definitely things that felt natural, more natural. It had been ten years since he'd lived here. And there was certainly enough change in that time that much of it felt different.

He pulled out his phone, flicking through his address book, but he had no contact info for anybody from his life before the navy, which was kind of sad. He thought about the friends he'd gone to school with, but most had left the area and had gone to make their fortunes somewhere else. Their parents were likely to be still around, but he wondered just how many people he would even remember.

When the cinnamon bun came, he looked at it and smiled. "Thank you." He picked up a fork and tried to break off a piece. It was so hot he didn't want to pick it up, but finally he gave up and picked up the monster and took a big bite. It was delicious. If he ever needed a sugar high, this would keep him going for days. The waitress stopped at his table and filled his coffee cup. "You new in town?"

"Back in town," he said. "Used to live here ten years ago, family still here."

She looked at him as if trying to recognize his face.

And then he looked at her and grinned. "Gail?"

She pulled out the empty chair beside him and sat down hard, a look of shocked surprise on her face. "Oh, my God, Blaze. I haven't seen you in …?"

"Ten years," he said. "I've been back and forth for visits, but I haven't done much socializing when I was here, preferring to spend all the time with my parents."

"I'm sorry about your mom," she said, the smile falling away to be replaced by grief. "She was really special."

"She really was," Blaze said. "And thank you. My mother lived a beautiful life. We all miss her, but she's gone, and there's nothing I can do but pick up the pieces and carry on."

"Good sentiment," Gail said with a smile. "So, you're the one who picked up Camilla then, are you?"

He pulled his eyebrows together. "And how would you know about that?"

"I saw Slim driving her car back to the recreation center where she was working. I talked to him when he came in for coffee, and he said she got a flat tire, and somebody brought her in, while Slim towed her car back."

"Yep, that was me. So, you're a local, from around here. I'm looking for a shepherd seen in the area. Have you seen it?"

"Sure, that big black one. Yeah, we wondered whose it was, and it comes and goes. You don't see it for a bit, and then you see it again."

"Do you remember the last time you saw her?"

"Probably a week or so ago?" she said, her gaze going out the window, as if looking inwardly. "I haven't ever stopped and tried to talk to her or nothing. I always wondered whose it was though."

"It's my mission to find and to help her if I can."

"Mission?" she pounced. "Is this a job then?"

"An unpaid job," he said with a grin. "A favor for a commander in the navy."

"Oh," she said, settling back. "Well, I hope something's done about the dog. I don't know what shape she's in. Every time I see her, she's running."

"I think that's all she knows how to do at this point. Running enough to stay alive."

She nodded. "That's what happens when you start running though, isn't it? You have to keep running because you don't know what to do, and you don't know if it's safe to stop."

"True enough," Blaze said, surprised at her insight. "So, what have you been doing for the last ten years?"

Just then the door opened, she looked up, and she chuckled. "Speak of the devil …"

He twisted to see Camilla walking in, her iPad in front of her, muttering to herself. He smiled. "Can I buy you a coffee?"

She looked up, but her gaze was unfocused. When she finally recognized who it was, her face lit up with a smile. "I should be buying you a coffee," she said.

Gail hopped to her feet. "I'll go grab a cup," she said, laughing. "You two can sort out who will pay."

Camilla took Gail's seat and looked at Gail's retreating back. "Do you two know each other?"

"We went to school together. I was just asking her about the shepherd you missed on the highway."

"I've mentioned it to a couple people too, and they all seem to think they've seen the same dog," she said, frowning. "If it keeps crossing that street, somebody'll hit it. I mean, obviously they don't want to," she said expansively with her hands. "I certainly didn't want to."

Nodding solemnly and holding back his mirth at her broken-tires discussion from yesterday, he said, "Slim was a good guy. Sounds like he still is."

"We'd be lost without him. Did you know he's the only locksmith in town too?"

"I didn't know that," he said, "but that's probably a good line for him."

"It's fine if you just want to rekey a door, and you're not

too worried if it's today or tomorrow," she said, "but, if you're locked out, and he's doing a tow job forty miles away, well, don't be expecting him to hurry back to unlock your house so you can get in."

"Speaking from personal experience, are you?" he asked, leaning forward, his tone gentle.

She glared at him. "It's not my fault I lost the keys to my house."

He could feel the chuckle starting inside again, but he managed to stay straight-faced and calm when he said, "No, of course not. I presume somebody else lost them?"

At that, she glared. "No," she said. "I live alone."

Confused, he said, "Well then, who lost them? Did your assistant misplace them?"

Her jaw dropped. "Why would you blame Blyth?"

He settled back with a sigh. "Instead of me making all these wild guesses, why don't you tell me how you lost them."

"Well, I put them down," she said.

He felt like he'd dropped down a rabbit hole. "Okay, so you're the one who lost them."

"Yes, of course." She stopped, frowned at him and said, "I just said that."

He wanted to roll his eyes but knew that wouldn't go over well.

Just then Gail returned with a cup of coffee and put it down in front of Camilla. She picked up the cream and dumped in a good portion, stirring it heavily.

"Looks like you've already had a busy day," he said.

Camilla nodded. "I'm more stressed because it's a wedding. I don't like doing weddings."

"I'm surprised you're in here."

She shot him a dark look. "I'm hiding. If my assistant knows I'm here, she'll be after me."

"So take her a cup of coffee back with you."

"I already did that this morning," she said, "but we have a thousand and one things to set up. I've got at least seven spots I'm supposed to hit right now."

"I'm sure you'll do fine. It'll all come together."

"It'll come together," she snapped. And then smiled and sat back. "I'm sorry. I don't need to be mean to you. I just get really stressed over weddings."

"When was the last one?"

"About three years ago," she said, "and it better be three more years before I do another one."

"It'll go off just fine," he announced. He had no clue if it would or not, but she obviously needed something to calm her down.

She took a big slug of the coffee and settled back with a smile. "That hit the spot." She looked at him. "So, did you look for the shepherd?"

He grinned at her. "I did. But, no, I didn't catch her. I think I caught a glimpse of her though. And might have found a way to tame her."

"How can you tame her if you can't catch her?" she asked with that supreme logic he had yet to figure out.

"We'll see," he said. "Do you need any help with your wedding this weekend?" He didn't even have a clue why he was offering because he was the least social person ever, and weddings and him did not get along. But then again, he'd only attended a couple, and they were for buddies. And they had actually been fun. He wasn't so sure about something that required a wedding planner. That sounded dangerously too highfalutin for him.

"We've got all that stuff under control," she said, frowning. "But it is nice of you to ask."

"Thank you." He picked up his coffee and nodded.

She looked at the plate beside him and said, "Did you have one of Gail's cinnamon buns?"

"Did she make them?" he asked in surprise. "Because I did, and it was divine. I should take one home to my dad."

"I'm sure he'd like that," she said. "I should tell you our mothers were not friends."

His lips quirked at hearing her repeat his father's earlier words. "Oh?"

Her shoulders sagged as he watched. "I wasn't going to say anything, but my mother phoned me last night and warned me to stay away from you, so I have this perverse need to go against her wishes."

He just stared, trying to process what she said and finding laughter bubbling up at the thought.

"I'm talking too much, aren't I?"

"It's not that you're talking too much," he said, holding his laughter in check, "but it's like you just say whatever comes to mind."

"Don't you?"

"Not really," he said slowly. "I tend to process and filter what I say, whereas you tend to just blurt it out."

She frowned and stirred her coffee cup again. He watched, seeing the coffee almost splash over the top. "It's fine, you know," he said gently. "I'm just used to people who are more worried about how they're received."

"I should probably guard my tongue more," she said, "but my mother has upset me, as usual."

"Does it matter to you if your mother wasn't friends with my mother?"

"I don't want it to matter," she said, "but the fact that I'm sitting here stirring my coffee as I am means it does."

"Okay. Do you always do what your mother tells you, or do you always do the opposite of what your mother tells you?"

She grinned, and then she chuckled. "I'm being foolish, aren't I? I'm almost thirty, and here my mom calls from the West Coast. She's already heard from her evil spies how you were back in town, and apparently, being Enid's son, you are the absolute worst person I could possibly spend time with, and she's horrified."

"Wow, she really didn't like my mother, did she?" He understood that. His mother was a lot of things, but she was a beautiful woman and very good at what she did, and that kind of grace and presence often spawned jealousy in others. "I'm sorry for your mother."

She looked at him, her jaw slowly dropping, and then she laughed. "Oh, my gosh," she said. "That's perfect."

He gave himself a slight head shake. "What's perfect?"

"That you feel sorry for my mother. Because she'd be so outraged to hear that."

He chuckled. "Then I guess it's a good thing she's not in the coffee shop with us, isn't it?"

She squeezed his hand and said, "Thank you. Now you've put my mother firmly in her place, and, in my mind, that works too."

Just then Gail returned with a coffeepot and refilled his coffee cup. As she topped up Camilla's, Camilla asked, "Can I get it to go, please? I really have to run."

"Of course you can." And Gail disappeared with Camilla's mug.

"You could have at least drunk that one and then taken

another one with you."

"I don't have time," Camilla said, pushing her chair back and standing. "The to-do list is just too long."

"If you get into trouble, and you need a hand, let me know." And he watched as she accepted the takeout cup and bolted out the door.

Gail looked at him with a wry grin. "So, I guess you're paying for coffee?"

At that, he laughed. "I guess I'm paying for coffee," he said with an agreeable nod. "Still, it's worth it. She does make me smile."

"Actually she makes all of us smile," Gail said with a wink, and she turned and headed back behind the counter.

CHAPTER 4

ONLY AS SHE walked into the rented center with her coffee did she realize that she hadn't paid for it. She groaned, wondering what Blaze must think of her.

"Is that coffee for me?"

"If you like it with double cream, yes," she hedged.

Blyth shot out her arm and said, "Today, for my midafternoon caffeine fix, I'll take it with double cream."

Camilla handed it over and carried on, but she wrote a note at the bottom of her tablet to thank Blaze as soon as she could. The trouble was, he had her contact information—but she hadn't collected his. Not very good on her part. But she did have Gail's contact. She fired off an email to Gail that said to apologize for her and that she'd pick up the tab next time. She should do it in person, but, right now, she was just too flustered and too busy to be bothered.

The next couple hours went by in a flash before she sagged into the closest chair and looked around. The dress rehearsal was tonight from eight to ten p.m., and then everybody was off to a fancy late dinner and drinks. Saturday, Camilla had to do more at the center, and then the wedding ceremony—which luckily Camilla was *not* in charge of—was Sunday morning, and the reception—which Camilla *was* in charge of—was Sunday noon through early evening. It was expected to be over between six and seven p.m.. But she'd often seen many of these die down and close up as soon as the bride and groom disappeared. She'd also seen many where the guests didn't leave for hours after the event was over. Lizzie and Brick were leaving somewhere around five o'clock, they'd said, maybe earlier if they could sneak away. Camilla could hope it would be earlier for everybody's sake.

"We have two hours until they get here," Blyth said.

Camilla looked at her. "What?"

"It's six o'clock. They'll be here in two hours, ready to start at eight."

She shook her head rapidly. "No, it's only one o'clock now," she said, lifting her iPad. She stared at it and then hit Refresh, realizing that, for whatever reason, the time on it had frozen. "Oh, my God, I thought we had hours yet."

"We do," Blyth said bracingly. "We have *two* hours left." She stopped in front of Camilla and said, "And really we're well in hand here."

"No, we're not. We still have to pick up all the flowers."

"They closed at six."

Just then her phone rang. It was the florist shop.

"I thought you were coming to pick these up tonight," Wanda said.

"I'm on my way. I'm on my way," Camilla said, running for the door.

"I'll drop them off on my way," Wanda said with a sigh. "You'll just have an accident if you try to race here. I'll be there in ten minutes." And she hung up.

Camilla, already halfway toward the front door, turned to look at Blyth and said, "We were supposed to pick them up a half hour ago."

"You didn't tell me that," Blyth said.

Camilla frowned, rubbed her temple. "What is happening to me?"

"You're not doing another wedding, period," Blyth said. "You're never like this except with weddings."

"I've only done a couple and didn't want to do this one. Wedding planners are expensive, and, as you know, Lizzie has one to handle the official ceremony in the park. Lizzie couldn't afford to hire that person for the rehearsal dinner and the reception too," she said, "though that's hardly any reason for me to step in."

"Two weddings, two maniacal temperaments to go with it," Blyth said. "So *no more weddings.*"

"I'm totally okay with that," Camilla said, "but somehow I have to get out of it when another friend decides to get married."

"Just say no," Blyth stated. "Have a couple referrals on hand to offer your friends instead."

Camilla nodded absentmindedly and took a deep breath. "We didn't even eat."

"We won't be eating for the next hour either. You're my best diet program ever," Blyth said in that ever-cheerful voice.

Camilla shook her head. "I'm so sorry. I didn't realize it was so late. We should have been done here hours ago."

"If it was anything but a wedding with its related events, we would be. Now let's get the rest of this done so, when the flowers arrive, we can put them out."

"We're only supposed to be getting some tonight, right?" Camilla knew the answer, but, since she'd lost track of time already, she didn't want to lose track of anything else.

"Yes, they wanted some of the flowers, and we're supposed to return them to the florist to keep them safe for

Sunday." Blyth added, "I don't even know why you have flowers for a rehearsal."

"You don't, but apparently this time we do because …" she said, "this bride wants it."

Just then she got a phone call from Lizzie, the bride in question. "I'm so excited. Is everything ready?"

"Well, it will be in an hour," Camilla said, rolling her eyes at Blyth.

"We're coming a little early," Lizzie said. "We want to make sure everything's set up just the way we want it." And with that, she hung up, still squealing with joy.

Camilla sagged even farther in the chair. "Lizzie's coming early," she said in a voice of doom.

"Oh, God," Blyth said. "Let's hurry."

Panicked, they finished the last of the mock setup here—because the wedding was at another site—and packed up their boxes, carrying them out of sight into the back room. She needed to invest in a truck or van for hauling items for her events. So far, being a smaller community delivery was included in the fees she paid, but it might be simpler to just buy a second vehicle. It was her frugal nature that was holding her back. Only sometimes that also got her into trouble. Up until now Blyth's old van had been a huge help when they got stuck. But that only worked for so long.

As they moved outside to await the florist's delivery and to not delay her any further, Wanda pulled up with the flowers. "I agreed to meet you back at the shop when this is over at ten p.m. to take possession of these flowers again, but this is the only time I'm doing this."

"I appreciate you doing that much," Camilla said. "But Lizzie wanted the flowers for tonight *and* Sunday, so short of having to order double the flowers …"

Wanda nodded. "I don't think there's anything more stressful than weddings. Better you than me for this one."

Camilla groaned, and they carried out the flowers.

They'd just gotten the last arrangement in position, Wanda gone already, when Lizzie pulled up with three other vehicles.

Her friend threw her arms around Camilla and hugged her. "I'm so excited," Lizzie said. "Can I go in? Can I go in?"

Camilla, her stomach sinking as she realized this really was the moment of truth, opened the doors and let her friend in. "Remember. This is just a sample for the rehearsal tonight," she said.

The crowd of ten streamed forward as Camilla and Blyth stood at the doorway. Camilla could hear everything, from excited squeals to silence to whispered concerns. Lizzie came back and said, "There'll be more flowers at the reception, right?"

"I told you this is just a few of the floral arrangements so you can get the main idea. I promise. There'll be a lot more at the actual reception."

"Good," she said, "and you got the pink baby's breath for my bouquet, right?"

"I believe so," she said, trusting in Wanda to pull that off. "I'll make a note to double-check with Wanda on that," and she pulled out her tablet and entered a note. She hoped that was enough to keep Lizzie glossing over to something else. Quickly she sent an email to Wanda on the pink issue.

"And we really don't like the centerpieces," Lizzie said, the words coming out in a rush. "I don't mean to insult you or anything."

Camilla looked at the long tables and started to chuckle. "Those aren't *your* centerpieces. Remember? This is a wedding rehearsal. We're not set up for the reception yet."

Her friend's face exploded in joy, and she threw her arms around Camilla again. "I knew you wouldn't let me down," she said, and she suddenly bolted.

Camilla called after her, "Hey, are you okay if we head out for the evening?"

"Absolutely," Lizzie said. "I'll call you when we're done."

"You need to," Camilla said. "We must collect the flowers and get them back into the proper temperature to keep them fresh for Sunday."

"I promise," Lizzie said soundly. Then her face cracked up in a big grin. "The problem with you planning the rest of my wedding weekend is I couldn't have you as part of the wedding party, but feel free to come to the rehearsal dinner tonight if you want."

"Honestly, I'm exhausted trying to make sure you have the best wedding rehearsal and reception possible," Camilla said warmly. "But thank you for the invite."

She didn't even think Lizzie heard her because she was gone already. Thankfully an email from Wanda came through with an affirmative on dyed pink baby's breath.

Blyth stepped up and said, "I don't know about you, but I'm ready to leave this place."

"Absolutely." Camilla turned to Blyth. "I know I asked you earlier, but I can't remember what you said. Did you have plans for tonight?"

"It's a Friday night. What do you think?" She toddled off to her old van and said, "I'll see you bright and early tomorrow morning." Just like that she was gone.

Weary, lugging still more boxes to her Mustang, Camilla finally loaded everything up, got into her car and was about to head home when a big black truck pulled up. She frowned as she watched Blaze get out.

He looked at the piles of stuff in the back seat of her car and said, "I gather you're done for the day?"

She nodded. "I'm done in every way possible. The rehearsal is about to start."

"Do you have to come back again tonight?" he asked.

She nodded. "Yes. I have to deal with the flowers."

"Interesting," was all he said.

She appreciated that. "What about the shepherd? Any news on that?"

"No. I stopped over at old Freddie's place, but he wouldn't open the door for me."

"Last time he talked to anybody was with a shotgun as punctuation," she announced. "He's pretty cranky these days."

"I just wonder if the shepherd is running from something. She seems to be very antipeople," he said.

"You haven't been here long enough to make that determination."

"True, that's very true," Blaze said in surprise. "However, I figured that, if you're as tired as you are, maybe you would like to go out for dinner." She stared at him in surprise, and he chuckled. "Or maybe we'll just call it a late lunch because I'm pretty sure you didn't eat that either."

HE WASN'T SURE how to take her reaction. She was interested yet wary. "We'll pick a public place," he said, "so you don't have to worry about anything out of the ordinary."

"It's not that," she said, "but I'm seriously exhausted."

"Fine," he said. "But consider this. What will you eat

when you go home?"

"I'm not sure," she said. "I don't think I have anything. I would probably pick up something and take it home."

"So, then we might as well go out instead," he said. "Pick a spot."

She shrugged. "I don't go out much so I'm not even sure what to suggest."

"You want fancy, or you want casual?"

"Casual," she said. "I feel dusty, dirty, tired and definitely don't want to go to a high-end place."

"Do they have very many high-end places in this town?" he asked.

"Yep, there are a couple," she admitted. "The town has grown. Oh, how about Italian? I don't know if you remember Mama Mia's."

He frowned as he tried to sort through the restaurants he knew. "I don't think I remember that name."

At that, she laughed. "In that case, that's where we're going. I can eat spaghetti off a spoon and not worry about people talking about my manners."

He shook his head at that, not sure who ate spaghetti with a spoon, but he was game. "Tell me how to get there," he said, "and I'll meet you."

"No, it's easier if I just drive and you follow me. I'm really lousy at directions." And, with that, she hopped into the front seat of her car and started up the Mustang.

He waited until she was almost ready to pull out of the parking spot before he got into the truck. He could imagine she was terrible with directions, but she seemed to be doing just fine with her business. He'd spent some time researching her, and she certainly had a lot of really nice reviews. Her prices were not on the website, and he worried she didn't charge enough for this kind of hand-holding. It had to be exhausting doing what she did.

From the look of her tonight, she was beyond that point. He hadn't planned to stop in until he saw her here as he drove by, and dinner seemed like the best idea yet. It was seven o'clock on a Friday night, and he didn't have any plans. He hadn't told his father where he was, but his dad was a big boy. Blaze contacted him as he drove, his phone on the seat beside him, and, when his dad answered, he said, "Hey, Dad. I'm taking Camilla out to Mama Mia's for dinner. I'll be back in a couple hours."

His father said, "Are you sure you're coming back tonight?"

"Absolutely," he said in a dry tone. "And, hey, you got any reason why that shepherd would be so skittish? I found a spot where I can feed her on a regular basis to try to get her used to humanity again, but I worry why she is almost ghostly out here."

"The only reason for that is if somebody doesn't want her around and has let her know very clearly she doesn't belong here."

"Not necessarily. She is a loner by nature. She might need time to bond with someone. She's also been alone for a long time, so maybe she wants companionship too. It's hard to know until I can get closer to her. Thankfully I didn't see a blood trail," Blaze said as he followed Camilla's car into the next turn. "But I am worried she might be wounded."

"It's a hard life for a dog on its own. They turn half wild. You know that."

"I understand, but I wonder if somebody is out hunting her or if she's just so skittish it'll take that much more time to catch her. Her file made it clear about her being a loner, so not sure what it'll take to get her to trust me."

"You know what? It's quite possible that whatever happened to her hurt her emotionally too. Once an animal bonds with somebody, you know it's hard on them when they lose that bond. Trust is something you have to earn with an animal and once broken, it can be hard for them to take the chance again. They are all heart and keep giving us the benefit of the doubt time and time again but at some point, it's too much and they retreat. If she's been half wild these last few months, food will go a long way to getting her to trust you. But depending on how skittish, it could take longer than you want."

"True enough," Blaze said. "I'll go back tomorrow morning and see if I can find her. I did leave dog food, and she did eat it, and I put a bit more down for her, but she's not responding well to me."

"Next time you can bring one of mine, maybe Anders here, and see how she responds to another dog. She's likely to take it either way, as positive or negative."

"That's something to consider. I don't know if she's against other animals or not. But something to think about." He rang off from the call and pulled into the parking lot of a small hole-in-the-wall front for a restaurant. It was an interesting choice she'd made, but she seemed pretty excited about it. He pulled up in one of those dinky-ass parking spots, wondering why, in a town where lots of people drove massive trucks, they never had spots large enough for them. When he hopped out, he grabbed his phone as he left. He locked up and turned to see Camilla standing at the front of the restaurant, waiting for him. "You didn't waste any time getting here."

"I decided I was really hungry," she said with a smile.

He opened the door and said, "Ladies first."

She raised an eyebrow but swept ahead in front of him. She wore jeans, some kind of a half boot, and a white T-shirt that may have started off white today, but it hadn't ended up that way. Also she had a shell-colored sweater over it. But it didn't matter what she wore, she stood with the same grace and attitude as somebody dressed to the nines. He appreciated that. Not that he believed she needed to be dressed up all the time. He had to admire somebody who could walk in with an attitude that said, *Take me as I am, and I don't care.* He was very much the same way; he was more comfortable in blue jeans.

CHAPTER 5

C AMILLA FORGOT HER state of clothing as she walked in, but, as soon as she saw the stares, her nose instinctively went up, and she followed the hostess as if she wore things like this out to dinner all the time. Truth of the matter was, she hadn't even given it a second thought, and she refused to think about anybody else's criticisms in the meantime. The only opinion that mattered was hers. And, well, maybe her date's. And how did that sound? She stole a glance at Blaze, happy to see he didn't appear to even notice. As they slid into the booth, and the candles were lit in front of them, she whispered, "I'm sorry I didn't get a chance to change."

"It doesn't matter to me," he said, his voice equally low. "I know you've been working, and a hot meal is exactly what you need, not a feeling of having done something wrong."

"My mother would be horrified," Camilla said with a nod of humor. "Appearances are everything."

"Appearances mean nothing," he said with a wave of his hand.

The waitress returned with menus. Blaze looked over at Camilla and asked, "Would you like a glass of wine?"

She smiled in delight. "Yes, I really would. It's been a very long day."

"Ditto," he said. He smiled at the waitress and said, "Could we also have the wine list, please?"

With a smile, she hurried off. He looked at the menu. "I can see seafood in my near future."

"Not sure about seafood and pasta," she said. "To be honest, I'm a big red meat eater." She felt his startled surprise, and she giggled. "I know. Everybody thinks I'm a rabbit eater," she said, "as in, I eat lettuce and salad greens. But I really do like my meat."

"Hey, so do I," he said. "What are you having then?"

"Spaghetti and meatballs," she announced. "Comes with big meatballs and lots of pasta, and honestly, I'm really hungry. And, if there's too much, I'll take it home for tomorrow."

"Will you get much chance to eat tomorrow?"

"No. The rehearsal is on right now, and they should be done anywhere between nine and ten," she said, waving her hand back and forth as she studied her cell phone with the time displayed. "So, we definitely have time for a nice relaxing dinner, and then who knows? If I'm lucky, the wedding party might leave early."

"It's hard to say, isn't it?" he said. "I imagine these things are unpredictable."

"Absolutely," she said, "but, hey, it's all good. It's a friend of mine, and I'm doing what I can to help her out."

"I'm surprised you're not part of the wedding party," he said, "or is she not that good a friend?"

She wrinkled her nose up at him. "It's a fine line, isn't it? The wedding party is generally reserved for best friends," she clarified. "And, if I was part of the wedding party, I'd have a hell of a time trying to organize these two events this weekend. I think she chose to demote me," she said with a chuckle, "in order to hire me."

"Are you good with that?"

"I'm so good with it," she said with a drawn look. "There's only so many weddings you really want to attend in your lifetime if they aren't yours. The more *other people's* weddings you attend, the questions get more direct, the looks get longer, and the *tuts, tuts* and the shakes of their heads become all too frequent from the guests and even the brides and grooms."

"Seriously?"

She nodded. "Particularly in my business when they see me arranging other people's weddings—another reason I can't stand doing them," she said, chuckling.

Just then the waitress returned with the wine list. "I'll give you two a moment to decide." And she stepped away.

"White or red?" he asked Camilla.

"I think it's supposed to be red with pasta, but honestly," she confessed, "I prefer white. Red puts me to sleep."

"Maybe that's what you need," he said, studying her features.

"Sure, that is what I need. Just not yet. I need to get the work done first."

"Is there much left to do?"

She nodded. "The flowers must get back into the cooler at the florist's, and everything at the center has to be cleaned up for something else happening there tomorrow, maybe a christening. I'm not sure."

"In a recreational center?"

She shrugged. "I don't remember what it was, but there is something."

"And then you clean it all out and redecorate it for Sunday?"

"Yes, originally she was supposed to rent the center for the entire weekend, but then she didn't want to pay for

Saturday, so she let that slide, and that meant somebody else could rent that day, and, well, it just created more work for everyone."

"Save a penny, spend a pound," he said with a sage nod.

"In this case many pounds," she said.

When the waitress returned, he picked out a white wine, one she'd never heard of, and ordered a carafe for them along with their meal choices.

After the waitress left them once more, Camilla warned, "Remember that I'm driving too."

"That's why the carafe," he said. "I figured we'll take the rest of the bottle, and you can have it tomorrow night or Sunday night when you're done."

"That would be lovely," she said. "Do they do that?"

"I have done it," he said. "You order the bottle but ask for only a carafe full at the moment."

"I'll have to remember that," she said. "I'll never object to taking leftover wine home either." She loved the way his grin flashed at her. She said suddenly, "I didn't realize your mom was the one in all those photos around town."

"Yes," he said. "My father mentioned you too."

"How is he doing?" she asked, skating over what his father might have said about her. The last thing she wanted to know was the details. It was probably just as twisted as everything her mother put out there.

"He's doing much better," Blaze said. "It's been tough picking up the reins after my mother's death, but it happens, so …" He shrugged. "Our choices are pretty minimal. Picking up the pieces is a requirement for continued living."

"I like the way you put that," she said. "It's hard when you lose somebody, but the fact of the matter is, life does go on, bills have to be paid, food has to be purchased, and somehow you're expected to do it all."

"So true," he said. "So true."

"You said something about coming here for the dog?"

"And to visit home again," he said, his gaze going over her shoulder to something she couldn't see.

"Are you planning on staying around?"

She watched him give a mental shake, and a small smile slipped out. "Maybe," he temporized. "I'm not sure yet. But I'd like to if I can make it work."

"Good enough," she said. "No pressure. Just wondered if you had a job or something here."

"No, I'm exactly the kind of man your mother would have warned you against," he said with a droll smile. "I'm not upwardly mobile, and I don't have stocks, full bank accounts or a fancy sports car."

She froze at the mention of her mother. "Did you mean that literally?" she asked in a careful voice. "Because most of the locals here know my mother expected me to marry up and to marry wealthy." From the shocked expression on his face and the apologetic look in his eyes, she realized it was just a common phrase. "I'm sorry," she rushed in. "I didn't mean to make that personal."

"I think that's my line," he said gently. "I didn't mean to make it personal, as in *your* mother."

"I don't know what to think about my mother at the moment. Apparently she really *hated* your mother."

"Why is that?" he said with a frown.

"My mother considers herself the most beautiful woman in the world," she said with a finger wave out to the rest of the world beyond their booth. "Not everyone agreed."

He started to chuckle. "I can tell you that my mother was as beautiful inside as she was out," he said warmly.

"And, from all that I saw, she was well loved by many."

"Yeah, my mother doesn't have that same fan base," Camilla said. "I'm not trying to speak badly of her, but she has made a lot of enemies."

"They used to say in the military," Blaze said, "you can judge a man by his enemies."

"Maybe," she said. "But I'd rather judge a woman by her friends."

"I like that too," he said.

They continued to exchange small talk until the waitress arrived with a bread board and a basket holding a hot loaf and a ceramic bowl of whipped butter.

Camilla lit up and reached for the bread the minute the waitress let go of it to leave their table. With the loaf in her hand, she said, "I was planning on sharing, you know?"

He laughed. Great big belly laughs that she watched in fascination. "How about I cut it," he said, "and then, if we really, truly finish it and need more, we can ask for another one?"

"I've done that too," she said, wrinkling her nose and leaning closer so only he could hear. "It's really good bread."

He picked up the knife and cut the small loaf into six slices. "There you go, three for you and three for me."

She took three and moved them closer to her and then dipped her butter knife into the butter keeper. "I really love bread and butter," she said. "My mother is forever telling me how it's carbs and how I shouldn't be eating them, but I gave up listening to her on that a long time ago."

"Carbs are a good source of energy," Blaze said. "As long as you're not watching your blood sugar levels, I don't see why you shouldn't be allowed to eat them. This looks like very good bread." He picked up a slice and sniffed the warm center.

"It is. They make it fresh here themselves. It's sourdough from Mama's old sourdough pot," she said, biting in, sagging back into her seat and closing her eyes as she ate. When she opened her eyes, he was staring at her, an odd look on his face. She blushed. "Sorry," she muttered, "but I really enjoy my food."

"Obviously," he said, his voice low and husky. "That's good to see."

She wasn't sure what that meant, but the air had subtly changed between them. It had been a long time since she last had a boyfriend. When younger, every boyfriend she brought home her sisters deliberately finagled out of her life and into theirs. It was almost as if whatever Camilla had, her sisters had to have. The competition continued after she got her inheritance, even when her sisters had moved to California, but now the breakups were the result of her mother's spies in town spreading gossip.

Camilla shook her head. Basically she had always had this problem with her sisters—until they both married. But Camilla had been celibate for way too long, and something about this man, his voice, touched her emotional core. The look in his gaze as it reached deep inside her belly and found the responding heat she'd never expected was ... surprising.

She straightened, buttered the second slice before the waitress came back with the carafe of wine and filled their glasses before slipping away. Immediately Camilla picked hers up and had a big drink. She put down her wineglass and realized she had drunk half the glass. She looked to Blaze to see a smile at the corner of his lips. "I'm sorry," she said abruptly.

And again his eyebrow shot skyward. "What are you

apologizing for now?"

She frowned and said, "I don't know, but I'm either fumbling and acting like a two-year-old or a spoiled brat, or … I just don't know. It feels very awkward all of a sudden."

"How about we go back five minutes to where you weren't feeling awkward."

Only five minutes ago, she felt a lot less awkward and a lot more heat. As in, if this restaurant had been empty, she might have crawled across this table and flattened him on the bench seat and had her way with him. Instantly that flashed through her mind, and she giggled.

He chuckled. "Now I really want to know what you're giggling about."

She shook her head. "Not happening," she muttered, shoving a large bite of bread into her mouth, chewing like the good chipmunk she was. To Camilla's relief, the waitress returned with large plates of food and promptly left. "It never ceases to amaze me how they can produce something like this time and time again, and it always tastes fantastic."

"Don't you arrange events time and time again, and it always turns out fantastic?"

She shook her head. "I try, and they'll be varying degrees of fantastic, but always? No. *Always* seems to be that word that just doesn't fit. It'll be the flowers that get screwed up, or the music didn't work out, or the speaker got sick or," she said, "any number of things happen."

"I think that's the same with cooking," he said. "They'll be short one can of tomatoes and use tomato paste instead. They'll finish with one brand of pasta and open a second one. They'll forget to salt the pot or not put enough in because they had to run and get another tub of salt." He shrugged. "Yet none of it matters in the end result." He looked down at his plate and smiled. "But they certainly didn't chintz on the seafood."

She studied his something-green pasta and asked, "Is that spinach pasta?"

"I hope so," he said, "and there are mussels and prawns, and it looks like scallops all through it. And in a cream sauce too." He dipped his fork into the cream sauce, tasted it and smiled. "With a bit of lemon and white pepper."

In spite of herself, she was intrigued. "I'm not terribly adventurous when it comes to food," she admitted, "but that does look good."

He twisted a couple noodles of fettuccine on his fork and said, "Here. Try this." And then he asked, "Scallop, mussel or prawn?"

"Prawn," she said.

The prawns were massive, so he cut one in thirds, poked the end of it with his fork and handed over the fork.

She hesitated and then shrugged. "My mother would, once again, be horrified."

"But your mother, once again, isn't here," he said gently.

She grinned, snatched the fork from his hand and popped the whole thing in her mouth. She returned his fork as she sat back, giving her mouth a chance to taste what had gone in. And she loved it. "Okay, I'm coming back next week, and I'm having your dish," she said.

"Good," he said. "And I'll have yours."

"Or," said the waitress, approaching them, "you can split your dishes half and half, and I'll bring you two spare plates." The waitress stopped and looked down at them. "You always have the same thing," she lightly scolded Camilla. "It would do you good to have something like that for a change."

"He just gave me a bite," Camilla said, nodding enthusiastically. "Oh, my gosh, it's so good."

"It is, indeed," the waitress said. "This time or next time?"

Regretfully Camilla said, "Next time. You know I come in here often. Just remind me next time."

"Will do," she said and hurried off to help somebody else.

"We could do that, you know?" Blaze said. "Tonight."

She shook her head. "No. It gives me an excuse to come back again."

"With me too, I hope," he asked with a woeful puppy-dog look as he admired her plate.

She chuckled. "You can come back tomorrow," she said. "I, on the other hand, will be putting together table settings and ornaments, and the front table all needs to be decorated."

"But you can't decorate tomorrow, can you?"

"No," she said. "Sunday morning."

They ate in joyful silence, both speaking minimally as they enjoyed their meal.

She was just about done when her phone rang. She glanced down and her eyebrow rose. "I wonder what that's all about."

"Don't you think it's the wedding rehearsal done early?" he asked. "It is nine."

"That would be too much luck," she said darkly. She answered the phone to hear Lizzie's voice, overexcited still, on the other end.

"Camilla, somebody threw a rock through the window," she cried. "We were right at the climactic moment," she said with so much melodrama it easily carried across to Blaze, who stared, fascinated, at Camilla's phone.

Camilla sighed and whispered, "She's very much a drama queen."

Lizzie continued, "I don't know if we can have the wedding reception here."

Camilla's heart froze. "What are you talking about?"

"You don't understand," Lizzie cried out, "like, the window's broken, smashed. It was horrible."

"Which window?" Camilla asked.

"The front one, right where we were standing."

Camilla frowned. "I'm just finishing dinner. I can be there in about ten minutes," she said. "I'll come and take a look."

"We've already left," Lizzie said. "I was way too upset to stay. So, we're going for drinks now before our dinner. I definitely need the drinks." She called out, "Ali, I want a few drinks first. My nerves are shot."

Lizzie, when she spoke again, was a little calmer. "You need to come up with a solution to this. I want my reception here. I don't want to move it somewhere else." And she hung up, just like that.

Camilla shook her head and laid down her phone. "Let's not even think about the fact I can't possibly rent any other place on such short notice, and let's blame the event planner for a hoodlum throwing rocks into the window when she wasn't even at the window. She would have been at the fake altar at the back wall. That's totally normal too, isn't it?" She sagged back in her chair and looked over at him. "So, it's back to work already."

Blaze had listened to that phone call, wincing at the demands the bride-to-be was making, wondering how Camilla could possibly want to work in this field. Of course she avoided weddings like a plague, and he could understand why. He couldn't imagine being single and having all these weddings to arrange with all those wedding mamas looking at her and tsk-tsking because Camilla was not capable of finding her own man. Just that thought would make his own stomach revolt. If his father even mentioned once about Blaze finding a partner, he knew he'd shut down that conversation in no time. "If you're ready," he said, "I'll go back with you."

"You don't need to," she said, gathering up her stuff. She looked over to see the waitress and raised her hand.

He hid a small smile because he was pretty sure her mother wouldn't like that I-need-the-check attitude of Camilla's either.

The waitress came with both checks, and, before Camilla could take hers, Blaze grabbed them both and placed a card down. "Charge them to my card, please."

Camilla hissed, "I can pay for my own."

"Yes, you can," he said, "but I invited you out, and, if I invite a lady out for dinner, I pay," he said firmly.

That made her sit back. But she didn't argue any further.

He signed the slip, accepted the receipt from the waitress and then said, "We don't want to forget the wine." The carafe was mostly empty, but he poured the last bit into Camilla's glass.

She picked it up and tossed it off with a smirk. "I needed that."

The waitress returned with the remains of the bottle and the leftover food from dinner. He accepted it and said,

"Come on, Camilla. Let's take a look at the damage."

She led the way back outside. As soon as she was out of the restaurant, she turned on him and said, "You don't have to come."

"Of course I don't, but what kind of guy would I be if I didn't, knowing the place was vandalized, it's dark out, everybody else has left, and you're checking it out alone? What if the hoodlum, as you called him, comes back?"

"Then I'll call the cops," she said crossly. She took several steps forward and then stopped, her back stiffening. But then suddenly her shoulders sagged, and she turned, and she said, "I'm sorry. I'm being a bitch. I had a lovely time at dinner. And thank you so much."

The switch from irate woman to genteel lady was so fast it caught him by surprise. He handed her the rest of the bottle and the leftovers, saying, "You can finish these when you get home, but right now we're heading to the center."

She nodded, hopped into her Mustang and took off.

He followed slightly slower. The lady liked speed, but he'd had enough speed in his lifetime. He'd seen the results of what happened when metal smashed against hard surfaces, and he'd heard the screams as limbs were torn off and friends were caught in fires. He'd been out in too many raids with bad endings. He accepted life at a much slower pace now, and he welcomed it. He pulled into the parking lot as she was getting out of her car. He got out and called, "Wait."

At the front door, she turned to look at him. "Why?"

"We should check the outside first."

She shrugged but was willing to let him take the lead. He walked to the obviously broken window. "You need to contact the landlord. See if we can get the window in tomorrow."

"Except the landlord, of course, won't answer since it's a weekend, and the window won't get a chance to be replaced tomorrow."

"Maybe, but there's another event, isn't there? And they may not want that window busted like this or boarded up."

She nodded. "I never even thought of that." She pulled out her cell phone, flicked through her contact list, hit the appropriate button and walked a few steps off to make the call.

He, on the other hand, stopped to take a look. It appeared a rock had gone through the upper portion of the large front-facing window. Jagged glass remained attached to the frame. He studied the window frame, decided it would be a fairly simple job—for two guys—to replace just the glass pane if that density was available locally. He peered inside and could see the rock on the floor. It wasn't a big rock. Therefore, either female or male could have hefted it. And it hadn't flown across the room, so again it could have been either sex. Several rocks were in the nearby garden, so it wasn't like the hoodlum was short on possible projectiles.

Now for the main question—was this an act of random violence? It was a Friday night in a small town, and he'd seen lots of kids get caught up in the moment, causing destructive forces. Or was this against Lizzie and her wedding, or was it against the landlord who owned the building, or was it a nebulous connection to Camilla herself? And would the law care? He turned to see her still talking on the phone. He walked over to the front door and propped it open, searching for a light switch.

With both double doors open, and the interior light on, he stopped at the entranceway and surveyed the damage. Again, it was just broken glass and a rock. Nothing inside had been damaged beyond a scratch on the hardwood floor. It was dark wood. If anybody had a walnut that could help hide the problem. He shoved his hands into his pockets and studied the interior. It appeared to be empty. His footsteps echoed in the dark. They had at least turned out the lights before they left. But he could see the flowers were still here, the ones that needed to be collected. He turned to look at Camilla's small Mustang, considered the number of flowers and shook his head. "No way they'll all fit."

She came up behind him and asked, "What won't fit?"

He motioned at the flowers. "All the flowers."

She frowned. "I have to get them to her place somehow. Maybe she'll come and pick them up. Although I know she's not happy about this in the first place."

"She likely already considered this issue. Call her now and see."

She shot him a disgusted look. "Doing that now," she said. She stood on the step and called Wanda—he could hear that conversation too. Wanda would be there in the next ten to fifteen minutes.

He started collecting the flowers at the farthest end but wasn't sure if the vases were supposed to come too. As she walked toward him, he asked, "Is the whole decoration going or just the flowers themselves?"

"The whole decoration," she said, "so the urns and the vases, all up and down this main section."

"Kind of ruins it to see it already, doesn't it?"

"A full-dress rehearsal will only show a portion of what the wedding does. And, if the bride insists, they can have the full wedding flowers set up too," she murmured. "Just whatever the bride wants."

"And does nobody else think that's a huge waste of

money?"

"Sure, we all do, but it's not our wedding," she said, "and that's where the difference is."

"I guess you've seen women turn from the nicest into the *worstest*," he said, deliberately mucking up the word.

"There's a reason the term Bridezilla was coined," she said over his chuckles. "But I've been basically lucky here, as my two brides have been pretty good. But it takes just one to remind you that you never, ever, ever want to do it again."

"And how is this one stacking up?"

"Middle of the road," she said, "except for this glass."

"What did the landlord say?"

"He's on his way. Depends if he can find somebody to fix it."

"Any auto glass place, if they do anything other than vehicles," he corrected, "should be able to fix it. The frame isn't damaged. The glass just needs to be removed and a new pane put in."

"So, like a new window?"

"No," he said, "a new pane of glass into the window frame."

She looked at him in surprise, glanced over at the window. "Are you sure?"

He chuckled. "Yes, I'm sure it's broken, but it's not destroyed."

"That might be easier then."

"A lot easier, particularly if you know anybody who deals in glass."

"Maybe," she said. "But I don't know if he's open tomorrow."

"The landlord might want to pay him extra to fix it first thing in the morning."

She nodded.

"Something we can ask him, for sure. He won't want to lose business," Blaze said, "particularly when he's got to fix this anyway. He might as well get it repaired and keep whatever business is booked tomorrow rather than losing the business and still having that expense."

"Well, I would," she said, "but I'm not so sure he'll care."

"Why is that?"

"Because he's seventy-five," she said. "And he's been considering selling the place, but, at the moment, it's pretty much his pension."

"Interesting," Blaze said.

"Or you could buy it," she said with a cheeky grin. "And then I can rent it from you."

"You probably only rent it a few weekends a year," he scoffed. "Under your current theory, what would I do with it the rest of the time?"

"The community college rents it for classes," she said, "everything from painting to music to English lit readings. I've often thought about buying it, but I just don't really want more businesses to handle."

"You'll need a business manager if you get into too much more."

Things got busy really quickly as the florist arrived, opening up the rear door of her van, and the flowers were collected, placed in the back, and she took off again, and she was no sooner gone than the landlord showed up.

He got out of his truck, took one look at the glass and frowned. "It's been a long time since I've had any damage like this," he announced. "It's hardly worth notifying my insurance company."

"If you know somebody who can do glass work," Blaze stepped in, "the pieces of glass can be removed from the frame and just a new pane put in."

"But they can't do that while the frame is in there, can they?"

"In theory, they might be able to. It depends what tools they have."

The landlord reached out a hand. "I'm Donnie. Who are you?"

Blaze smiled, introduced himself and said, "I'm Dex's son."

"That makes you Enid's boy," he said with a big grin. "You're a fine sight for sore eyes."

"Thank you," Blaze said. "I know my dad's happy to see me."

"You were sidelined in the military for a medical discharge, weren't you? Didn't I hear something about that?"

Aware of Camilla's sudden look, he nodded. "Yes, things went wrong on a mission. It took a couple years to get back on my feet."

"I bet," Donnie said. "Glad to have you home though. Have you figured out what you'll do while you're here?"

"Nope, not a clue," he said with a grin. "Now back to this glass."

"Yeah, Scottie's Glass. He fixes all kinds of things, including windshields. He's an auto glass guy, but, in a small town like this, you know, one has to do what one can, so he tends to do windows too. He could order me a new window but …"

"Well, we can certainly clean up all the shattered glass, but then it leaves an open pane," Blaze said. "It's a hot summer day. Maybe that would be okay for a day or two.

The other thing is, if Scottie came and took a look at it, got some measurements, he probably could fit it with a new piece of glass in the morning."

"Maybe. I'll give him a shout," Donnie said, muttering. He walked back to his truck and pulled out something, and he searched through what looked like an address book.

Camilla whispered, "He's old-school."

"That's all right," Blaze said. "People move forward in technology at their own speed. And, if they don't ever make it, they don't ever make it." She looked at him in surprise, and he just smiled. "I have great respect for the elderly."

"Good," she said. "Very few do."

He looked around and said, "So does anybody call the law over this? You called the florist and the landlord, but does anybody call the police?"

"What's the point?" Donnie asked. "I'll stop by and tell them somebody threw a rock through the window, and he'll write up an incident report, but we don't have any suspects, and they're long gone now."

"True," Blaze said. He motioned at the footprints in the lawn. "There are footprints around."

"Yep, but we've all walked through here by now," Camilla said, "and I'm sure Lizzie's bridal party did too."

Blaze nodded. "Too bad if they did because some of these prints would help identify the suspect."

"You still need a suspect to match them up to," Donnie said. "Scott's coming and taking a close look in the morning. He does have glass, and he might be able to fit one in."

"Perfect," Camilla cried out. "I do love to hear that. That's the thing about small towns. Everybody tends to help each other."

Blaze wondered about that because somebody from a

small town had done the opposite—but why?

Donnie turned back to Camilla and said, "Hopefully this should be done before your deal on Sunday."

"Right," she said. "It needs to be. The bride is already pretty upset."

"Did you ever check that the kitchen dishwasher was working?"

Her face fell. "No, I never did."

Blaze followed along behind them, his gaze looking at the huge space. It had been partially set up for the wedding rehearsal, but a lot of the tables and chairs were still in place for general usage. In the back was a large kitchen with two fridges and a couple stoves. "Do you rent this out for any type of event?"

"We've had everything from pet grooming classes to cooking classes in here," Donnie said. "There aren't many spaces like it. And, as Camilla here knows, since she arranges the only conventions in town, this is the largest space available."

"It is, indeed," she said. She marched to the dishwasher, played with the knobs and then turned it on. Immediately they could hear water running through it. She switched through several different cycles and then opened it. "It looks like it's working," she said. "Did you get somebody in here?"

Donnie nodded. "But they didn't send me an invoice, so I wasn't sure if he'd done any work or not." He stared at the dishwasher critically. "It doesn't have too many more years in it."

"As long as it doesn't die on one of the days I've got it rented," Camilla said, chuckling.

At that, he just sighed. "Another expense," he muttered.

"But one that makes you money," Blaze said, his voice

quiet.

Donnie nodded but didn't say anything else.

They headed to the front, and Donnie locked the door. He walked to his truck and got in, gave them a light honk and drove away.

Camilla smiled up at Blaze. "I really did enjoy dinner, so thank you. Now I'm taking the leftovers and that remaining bottle of wine and going home. I need a good night's sleep. I have all of the table prep to do for Lizzie's reception." At his blank look, she just shrugged and said, "Have you ever been to a wedding?"

He nodded. "Several of my friends."

"Were there like candles and flowers and ornaments on all the tables?"

"Yeah, all kinds of stuff," he said, "especially the front table where the wedding party sat."

"Exactly," she said emphatically. "So I'll make sure all those table toppings get made tomorrow." She hopped in her Mustang and said, "Goodbye," and she took off.

He stood here for a long moment, his hands thrust into his pockets, wondering how he suddenly found himself all alone on a Friday night. He certainly hadn't expected to take her home. But he hadn't expected such a quick end to their night together. He looked around the parking lot, wondering if there were any cameras. He should have asked Donnie when he was here. But, from what Blaze could see, there weren't any. Nor any security. In a big city that would never be allowed. Without security, the buildings would be covered in graffiti, and that cost a small fortune to clean up. He still didn't understand why this building would have been targeted. He walked the perimeter again, surveying the area and the building itself.

There wasn't anything to really see, but it made him wonder. The center was the only place on the block, so it wasn't like the rock-throwing was a random act. Somebody was here, walking down the street, and decided to break a window—or the music or laughter or sounds of happy people had triggered an odd reaction, and the hoodlum decided to disrupt the wedding festivities. And that was possible too.

It was dark, but Blaze wondered about the shepherd, and, since he wasn't quite ready to go home, he got in his truck, drove to where he'd last left the food. It was gone. *Good*, he thought. He placed more food in the same spot and sat down on the ground, calling out to her. "Easy, girl. Come on. Isn't it time to just come home? I won't hurt you. I know you've had a pretty rough life."

He could hear the bush crackling off to the right, but he didn't move. He just kept calling her in that same soft voice.

Eventually he let his voice die away, and he sat here, leaning against the tree. Darkness settled in, and he sniffed the air. Just like she knew he was close by, he could smell her too. "I'd really rather you came and said hi," he said. "I don't intend to hurt you."

When he opened his eyes, golden eyes stared at him. He smiled. "Hello there."

The dog took one step forward, but, when a vehicle drove down the road, she bolted. Slowly Blaze climbed to his feet, knowing it was the end of that for the night. The vehicle had scared off Solo and had scared her off good. It was time for him to go home too.

Still, she'd approached him, and that made his efforts all worthwhile.

CHAPTER 6

W HEN CAMILLA WOKE the next morning, she checked her watch and groaned. It was only six a.m. She never woke this early. She lay in bed, realizing something had woken her. An odd howl drifted her way. She slowly sat up and walked over to the window. She could see someone fleeing in the distance, but they were too far away to see who it was. From her window she couldn't see much but she swore she saw a dog slink into the trees… but as she peered closer she had to wonder if she'd mistaken it.

Not liking this, she pulled on a bathrobe and stepped into slippers and cautiously walked downstairs. Her mom and sisters would be screaming at her for not calling the cops first, but, if somebody was running away from her house, she couldn't imagine what she would find downstairs.

As she arrived in the kitchen, she groaned to see one pane of her French doors shattered by a rock. One rock, and it was still inside on her kitchen tile floor. Her house had a Mediterranean flavor with all orange-gold tiles on the floors and its high ceilings. It had been her grandmother's house. Her grandmother had loved spending most of her life in Italy with her many lovers, and, when she retired, she decided to bring that same flavor back home with her.

Camilla stared at the rock, wondering why and how somebody had gotten in her yard. She had a gate across the driveway, so they hadn't driven in. On that note, she finally found her feet and raced to the front door, flinging it open. But she'd missed seeing the vehicle, was too late, or there hadn't been one, because the front gates were visible and nothing was parked outside them. She thought about where she'd seen the intruder running to—off in an angle to the side of her backyard where the cedar hedges were. Although she had partial fencing, the cedars did a good job of keeping the unfenced part enclosed. But she had noticed a couple hollows showing up. The last thing she wanted to deal with right now in the middle of wedding weekend was the expense of trying to fence the rest of her backyard—but also because it would mean likely uprooting the cedars there.

She slowly moved back into the kitchen, wondering what she was supposed to do. Obviously she would talk to Scott. This was a little more serious than the window at the center—that broken pane had been high up; this one was level with her door handle; plus this was her home, not some rented center. And this was also much more directed at her. Finally she called the sheriff, not wanting to wake him, but, at the same time, she didn't want to deal with this alone.

"What's the matter, Camilla?" The sheriff's rough voice came on the phone.

"Somebody just threw a rock through my French door," she said. "The kitchen floor is covered in glass."

"What?"

"Yeah," she said, her voice quiet. "And I don't know if Donnie called you or not, but somebody threw a rock through the rec center last night too."

"Same person?" he asked, but at least he sounded more awake.

"I have no clue. I did see somebody dressed all in black

running off my property, but I couldn't possibly give you a description except tall, thin and wearing all black. I didn't see any vehicle. Why would somebody do this?" she snapped. "Like I need this headache."

"Of course you don't," he said in a soothing voice. "Did you piss anybody off lately?"

"No more than usual," she said, running her fingers through her hair. "And there's not enough coffee in the world to make me look at this and feel good about it."

"I'll get dressed and put on some coffee myself," he said, "and then I'll come on over."

"Fine," she said and hung up. She tossed her phone on the counter, wondering why the security alarm hadn't gone off. And then realized she'd been so tired last night that she hadn't set it. She knew she wouldn't forget it again. She put on coffee, and her phone rang.

"Are you all right?" Blaze's voice came through the phone loud and clear.

"What's the matter?" she asked. "You precognitive now?"

There was silence on the end of the phone. "No," he said, "my dad was just talking to the sheriff. And apparently your place got broken into?"

"That's an exaggeration. Somebody threw a rock through the French door. I thought for sure my alarms would have gone off, but I forgot to set them."

She could feel the disapproving silence on the other end. She frowned at her phone. "You can't tell me off. I'm already telling myself off," she said crossly. "One of us is enough." And she hung up her phone. She needed coffee before she dealt with anybody else, so, if anybody called now, that was too bad—she wasn't answering. As soon as she had coffee dripping and she could smell the aroma, she felt a little calmer. But her mind raced with questions as to why. And who?

Finally she poured herself a cup and headed out to the front where she sat down on the porch bench. She had already opened the gate, figuring the sheriff would be here soon. Instead, a big black truck she recognized arrived. She stood, shaking her head, only now realizing she hadn't even gotten dressed.

Blaze hopped out. "Are you okay?"

She raised both hands in frustration. "Outside of being pissed, yes, of course I am. Go ahead and take a look, see if you can make any sense of it."

And he disappeared in the house.

She sat back down again with her coffee. She really didn't want to deal with the sheriff either while she was in her pajamas. When Blaze didn't come back out, she headed inside to find him sipping a cup of her coffee as he stared at the glass. "So, did you just come here for coffee?" she asked caustically.

"No," he said. "I want to know the connection between you and that center."

"Of course the connection is that I rent it," she said, "but that has never been worth throwing rocks and breaking windows before. And why did the sheriff call you?"

"The sheriff called my dad," he said. "You won't like the reason either."

"Why is that?"

"Because the sheriff talked to Donnie, and somebody else had called Donnie, once they heard about the broken window, and said they'd seen a black truck outside the place earlier when nobody was around."

She looked at him in confusion. "Of course. You were there."

"Exactly, and that was what this caller told Donnie. That I was there for *sinister reasons.*"

"To break the window at the rec center?" She shook her head. "Why? What do you care?"

"Exactly. I'm also tall and slim, and I wear a lot of black."

She looked at him in surprise, then noted he wore black jeans and a black hoodie. "You are, and you do," she said, "but you're not who I saw running away earlier."

"How do you know?" he asked.

"Your shoulders are bigger, and I would imagine you run more like an athlete, although I haven't ever seen you run. This person sprinted but not like they were used to doing much running." She frowned. "I don't have a clue why I said that."

"Because first impressions are very important. I presume he wore a hoodie with the hood up?" He put his coffee down and pulled the hood over his head.

She turned to stand behind him and nodded. "I was up in my bedroom, and I could see it." She hesitated.

He waited.

"You're going to think I'm crazy but I thought I heard a howl, like a dog warning me. That's how I woke up. I know it's probably my imagination but I might have seen a shepherd slink off into the trees on the other side from where the intruder had been. But it happened so fast, and it was hard to see in that light ..."

Surprise lit his gaze. "Interesting. It could have been Solo. Unfortunately for her, she was aptly named." He motioned at the hallway behind him. "Come on. Take me to your room and show me the window and where he was running to."

She led the way upstairs and pointed out from her bedroom window where she'd seen the intruder. "You can still see his tracks somewhat."

"I'll be right back." Blaze went out the balcony and down the stairs that she had right there from her master bedroom.

While he was gone, she changed into leggings and a long T-shirt. She picked up her coffee and headed back downstairs again, seeing the sheriff coming in through the front door. The sheriff looked at the truck and frowned.

"Yes, that's a black truck," she said. "Yes, there was a black truck at the center last night. But it's Blaze's truck, and he was with me."

"It was mentioned to Donnie that nobody else was at the parking lot."

"Blaze and I left there, went for dinner at Mama Mia's and came back again, and that's when we found the rock smashed through the center's front window."

"Oh," the sheriff said, pushing his hat back and scratching his head. "So why would somebody try to make it look like it was Blaze?"

She shrugged. "Because he's the new guy in town? If somebody wants to cause trouble, well, he looks like a nice choice for a fall guy?"

"No idea why though," he said. "Blaze has been around here for a lot of years. Don't make no sense."

She led the sheriff into her kitchen so he could take a look at the broken window pane on her French door. He walked around and then said, "You better give Scott a call."

"Yes, I'll do that."

"You got insurance?"

"Yes, I have insurance," she said. "But it might not be worth the deductible to just get the door fixed."

"Unless the door has to be replaced," the sheriff said. "Then you're looking at a couple thousand."

She winced at that. "Well, let's hope it doesn't. I'm trying to stick to a budget."

"Hence the insurance," the sheriff said, looking at her.

Hearing something, they both looked into the backyard to see Blaze coming through the separating hedges and toward them. "Black pants, black hoodie," the sheriff said in a neutral tone. "You sure it wasn't him?"

"Positive," she said firmly. "Just look at him. Broad shoulders, athletic hips. But this person I saw in my yard was tall and skinny with narrow shoulders, and looked like running wasn't necessarily something he was prepared to do, but he could certainly sprint for a short distance," she admitted. "I sent Blaze to check out where I saw the intruder disappear to."

"You don't know much about Blaze. Remember that," the sheriff cautioned.

"I know," she said. And she flashed him a bright grin. "But what I do know, I like."

He chuckled. "I know his dad, and his dad is good people, and Blaze used to be good people. But I also know that sometimes, when the men and women come back from service, they're different."

"I just heard last night," she said, "that he returned with a medical discharge."

"Yeah, none of the family talks about it much. But apparently Blaze went through a pretty rough time. That's why he didn't make it to his mom's funeral. He couldn't travel."

"Ouch," she gasped softly. "That would have been very difficult."

"For everybody involved," the sheriff said calmly. They waited in silence for Blaze to reach them, the sheriff opening the back door for him. "Did you see anything, son?"

Blaze shook his head. "Just vehicle tracks parked back there, which took off very quickly and sprayed tons of gravel all over the road."

"Well, that would make sense," the sheriff said. "Trying to get the hell away."

"But why just throw a rock?" Blaze asked. "Once you've thrown the rock, don't you hang around and see what people do, or don't you try to come in and take something?"

"Or it was just vandalism?"

"Then why all the way around to the back of the kitchen?" Blaze questioned.

"Because they can't be seen from that side," Camilla said suddenly. "It's the one area that's not open to view from the road."

The men studied the road that curved around her place and confirmed that she was right.

"But they still took a chance," Blaze said thoughtfully. "Something more is behind this."

"I don't think I want to know what," she said quietly. "As far as I'm concerned, this is bad enough."

"It's nuisance value only," the sheriff said slowly. "I can't see any reasonable explanation."

She looked over at the sheriff and said, "You got an anonymous tip about a black truck somewhere out here close by?"

He nodded.

"Yeah, mine," Blaze said, "but it's hardly like I've been

out here throwing rocks at windows."

"Of course you haven't," Camilla said warmly. "I've been with you the whole time."

"Well, not quite," he said. "But you've certainly been with me before and after we learned about the broken window at the rec center, and you saw me just arrive here and now."

"Exactly," she said. "This makes no sense."

"Unless somebody's trying to make it look like it was Blaze," the sheriff said. "I can't help noticing you're wearing black jeans and a black sweatshirt with a hood."

"Yeah, and that's what the person who threw the rock was wearing apparently too," Blaze said. "So that's a consideration, but it's obvious I wasn't here, and we now have another perpetrator."

Camilla's phone dinged at that moment, and she snatched it up, swiped to take a look at the message and then frowned. "*Stay away from him,*" she read out loud. As she scrolled down, she saw images of Blaze. Blaze from a few years ago maybe. She held it up and said, "Recognize that?"

He took the phone from her hand and frowned at it. "Sure, it's me," he said. "A few years ago though, like ten maybe." He handed it back to her. "Who sent it?"

She scrolled up to see the email address and then said, "From besthappinessinterest@hotmail.com," she said drily. She handed it over to the sheriff. "What the hell's going on?"

"Sounds like you've got a stalker," he said slowly. "Somebody who doesn't want you to get too close to Blaze here. Particularly if that message is anything to go by."

"*Stay away from him*? That almost sounds like a jealous girlfriend," she said, her gaze going to Blaze. "Did you leave behind a trail of broken hearts when you went off to the navy?"

He leaned against the kitchen doorframe, his arms across his chest and shook his head. "No, I sure didn't, and, even if I did, that was ten years ago. Who cares now?"

"Well, it depends if you left behind a pregnant teenager or some other such thing," Camilla said, studying his face. Camilla thought he looked uncomfortable at the line of questioning, but then it was very private and very disconcerting. He did *not* look guilty.

He shook his head. "To the best of my knowledge I have no children anywhere," he said coolly. "And I get that maybe my return has disturbed some people's peace of mind, but I wouldn't know who, and I wouldn't know why."

"Were you involved in anything before you went away?"

He shook his head. "No, and I didn't leave under a dark cloud either. I was accepted into the navy, and I left. That was the end of it. I've been back several times to visit while on leave, and I haven't been back since about four months before my mother's death."

"That's right. You didn't make it for the funeral." The sheriff slipped his hands in his pockets and rocked back and forth on his heels as if thinking about that and trying not to pass judgment.

Then Camilla figured he was just looking for confirmation of their earlier conversation.

"I was in my own hospital bed at the time," Blaze said quietly. "I wasn't mobile enough to be released from the VA hospital."

The sheriff nodded quietly. "I remember your father saying something about that."

"But still, this is pretty petty, and it's obviously not well-thought-out," Camilla said. "I mean, I saw the person running away." She didn't mention the dog to the sheriff but was dying to ask Blaze if he'd seen Solo out there—or any sign she might have been the dog Camilla thought she'd seen.

"I know," Blaze said. "Of course you and I had dinner together last night, but what's the chance that whoever is doing this didn't know that?"

She frowned. "Well, it's possible. Normally I would have gone straight home. In fact, I did tell everybody I was going home."

"Who did you tell?" the sheriff asked.

"Blyth, for one," she said. "My assistant. And Lizzie's wedding party as they invited me out for drinks with them, but I just wanted to go home," she said with a wry smile. "I didn't tell anybody Blaze and I were going out for dinner together."

"Sure, but anybody in the restaurant could have seen us," Blaze said.

"True enough," she said with a tilt of her head. "We weren't trying to keep it secret."

"No, but somebody has been alerted to the fact that potentially you're dating, and they are not happy about it," the sheriff said with a frown. "This can get pretty ugly. I don't want to see it going in that direction."

"Neither do I," Blaze said. "But now that her stalker has this in their head, what's the chance that even me staying away from her will make it stop?"

"It's hard to say," the sheriff said. "If that's what he wants you to do, it might be enough."

"I don't care if it is or not," Camilla snapped. "I go out with whoever the hell I want to go out with. Throwing rocks in my kitchen door, like, what's with that?"

"I don't know," Blaze said. "Except that it was something they could do. An outlet for rage. Better than taking a rock and smashing you."

At that, she could feel her blood thin and her limbs get cold. "Are you saying I'm likely to be attacked next?" she asked in a low voice, searching both men's faces. But what she found there did not invite confidence.

"Anything is possible," the sheriff said with a nod. "This isn't normal. I wouldn't have tied the two rock-throwing incidents together until we got that email. … Well, except for the timing."

"If they had thrown the rock at something else," Blaze said, "God forbid, your Mustang, while it was parked downtown or something, then it could have still been random. But, to come to your house, it's very specifically targeted at you."

She walked back into the kitchen to put on another small pot of coffee. She stared down at the coffeemaker while it dripped. When it was finally done, she filled her cup and turned to look at the others. Nobody had said a word for the last five minutes.

Blaze held out his cup, and the sheriff nodded. She filled one up for him too and said, "So, now what?"

"Now you watch out," Blaze said before the sheriff could. "Now you look at everybody sideways, wondering who would do this and who sees you in an odd light, either as a suitor or maybe a frustrated stalker."

She stared at Blaze blankly. "I thought this was about you, as the newcomer," she said with a small cry. "I thought it was about you being either dangerous or …"

He stiffened and then shrugged. "That's another possibility too. I wasn't really thinking that."

"How can we not?" the sheriff asked. "'Stay away from him' can mean either that somebody wants Camilla to himself or that someone is afraid you'll hurt her."

"Or," he said, "it's got nothing to do with me, and this guy's just a crazy-ass lunatic."

"That's all too possible too," the sheriff said. "As we well know, these situations can get difficult, and we lack answers. At the moment, literally just stay safe. Don't go out alone, look after yourself. If you get any more weird incidences like this, then give me a shout." He put down his empty coffee cup and headed outside.

"Aren't you going to look for fingerprints or anything?" Camilla asked.

"Fingerprints? The only thing to fingerprint would be that rock," the sheriff said, "and do you think they had gloves on?"

"Yes, I do think so," she said, "but I couldn't be sure of that."

"Well," Blaze noted with a head tilt toward the sheriff, "considering the fact I'm standing here without gloves on, and you saw him with gloves on, you can see again it wasn't me."

She nodded.

As the sheriff walked away, the rock now in a plastic bag, she said, "If you get any fingerprints off it, let me know."

"I can if there's anything to get off," he said. "I'll try, but there still has to be somebody to match them to."

"I'm thinking you should collect the rock from the rec center too," Blaze said.

"Will do," the sheriff said. "I'm on my way over there now." He took his leave.

Blaze turned to her and said, "Do you know anybody

who would be against the two of us going out on a date?"

"I've been thinking about that," she said, turning and walking back to the coffeepot. She stared down at it, saying, "I really don't need more coffee, but I want it."

"Sometimes having the coffee is more about comfort than it is about caffeine," he added gently. "But, if you can talk to me, maybe we can figure this thing out."

"I'd love to," she said, "but are we really thinking a rock through the center last night was intended to hurt me?"

"No," he said. "Intended to hurt your business or intended to put you off me," he said. "Not trying to hurt you physically, and I don't think that's the direction this is going but more about keeping you away from me."

"I guess"—her voice fell short as she was lost for words—"I guess the only way to know depends on what he does next. From the *Stay away from him* email, I would say he's *not* trying to hurt my business, but last night's rock through the center *does* try to hurt my business."

"Unless that was sheer frustration," he said slowly. "If people had heard I was in town and happened to see me there."

"That's possible," she said. "But somebody must have a longstanding feud to see you and have it suddenly triggered again now that you're in town," she said. "So I'm back to thinking this is more about you than it is about me."

"And that's possible," he said.

IT WAS POSSIBLE, but he didn't know how as he hadn't left with any bad feelings from anyone as far as he knew. He'd had a girlfriend, but they had broken up amicably a long time ago, and she was currently married with several chil-dren. Although he hadn't looked her up, he planned to. She'd married a guy he'd known in high school and had been good friends with. It wasn't like he wished either of them ill—Blaze couldn't imagine her husband giving a damn about Blaze either. He shook his head. "I know what you're saying," he said, "but it doesn't make any sense. Why don't we shelve the entire problem for now? And, if you've got lots of work to do, and I know it's still really early in the morn-ing, maybe I can help you."

She shook her head. "The last thing you want to do is sit here and fold napkins in fancy ways and tie ribbons around candlesticks and put rocks into jars, and that's just for starters."

He swallowed hard at that. "No, can't imagine I would," he said. "I would much rather clean up this glass and take measurements and run down to Scottie's Glass and see if we can get a new glass panel to fix this door."

She brightened. "Would you do that?"

He looked at her in surprise. "Absolutely."

She said, "Perfect. I'll even fix you breakfast then."

"That works," he said, "just point me to a broom and a tool kit." He grabbed the broom she handed him and carefully cleaned up all the glass inside and outside of the shattered door.

She stood around, like at a loss for something to do—or not knowing what to do next.

"Here," he said, pulling out a chair to her breakfast nook. "Sit down with your coffee and relax a bit before getting back to work." And then, rummaging around in her hall closet for the few tools she had, he grabbed the pliers and carefully pulled all the remaining broken glass from the frame. The frame was one that came apart. He took careful measurements, wrote them down, took out a piece of the frame and turned to look at her. "I can take this down to Scott's when I go and see if we can get something to fit."

She nodded and smiled. "I really appreciate this," she said.

"No problem. Are you feeling better?"

She looked at him blankly, then smiled. "Yeah, I guess. So how about breakfast?"

"What have you got?"

"Not a whole lot," she confessed, opening the fridge. "I haven't shopped in a few days." He looked over her shoulder to see eggs and not a whole lot else. "Well then, how about eggs?"

She laughed. "If we're lucky, there's bread here too." She pulled out her bread drawer and spied a few pieces of salvageable bread and half a bun. She cried out in dismay. "Maybe not," she said, "those look pretty sad."

"Do you have any potatoes?" he asked.

"Maybe a couple. Why?"

He shook his head and said, "You want to check?"

They walked over to the pantry and there, beside the onions, were two potatoes.

He snatched them up. "Perfect. Do you have a grater?"

She looked at him suspiciously. "So you'll be cooking now? What are you thinking of making?"

"You obviously like potatoes or you wouldn't have them in the house," he said, "so why don't you just wait and see?"

She seemed happy with that. She pulled out the eggs while he grated the potatoes. He let her watch as he seasoned them, drained off some liquid, added an egg and some flour. He then took two fry pans and made two mid-size patties in the center of each. He fried them up gently on a moderate heat until they were golden brown and flipped them and cooked them for another few minutes. As soon as they were done, he moved the patties off to the side of the pans and cracked eggs in both pans.

He glance over at her then chuckled at the look of astonishment on her face.

"I can cook, but I don't do anything very adventuresome."

"This is hardly adventuresome," he said. "It's just basics." And before long, he flipped them onto plates, and they had hash brown patties and two fried eggs.

They sat down together. He watched as she dove into the potato pancake.

"This is lovely," she said around the food in her mouth. "Really nice and crispy."

He ate a little slower than she did, and, when she was halfway done, she stopped, looked at him and his plate and said, "I feel like I'm inhaling my food, and you're dawdling."

"Savoring," he said. "I'm really enjoying the potatoes."

That had her slowing down. By the time they finished, she sat back, rubbed her tummy and said, "Okay, I feel much better now."

"Food does that," he said. "Now, let's clean up the kitchen. I'll take a trip into town to talk to Scott."

"Good enough. Blyth will be here soon, since we have all this stuff to do."

He looked around and said, "I don't understand where the stuff is." He rinsed his plate and loaded it into her dishwasher. "By the way, I did look but couldn't see any tracks from the dog on the lawn. Still, I think it's possible from the tracks on the other side that Solo is hanging around your place." Finishing wiping the counter, he turned and said, "So where is the 'stuff to do?"

"Come this way, and I'll show you." She led him through the first floor to almost a ballroom-size room. Not quite, of course, but it had lots of tables, and it was filled with boxes.

He nodded. "This is a great space for what you need to do."

"Absolutely," she said. "This was my grandmother's house. I've always loved it."

"And it's yours now?" he asked.

"You'll hear the rumors anyway," she said, "so I might as well tell you up front. I inherited a lot of money and the house from my grandmother."

"Good," he said. "It's not like she could take it with her."

With that, she laughed out loud. "So true," she said. "You sound like Grandma. She taught me to be frugal, to save for a rainy day, that money is a tool, not the end goal. But my mother and two sisters, although they got an inheritance from my grandmother, they didn't get anything like what I got," she confessed. "There are definitely still some hard feelings."

"Is your mother her daughter?"

Camilla shook her head. "No, Grandma was her mother-in-law. And they never got along."

"Well, that she got something is amazing," he said.

"Yeah, I think it was more done as an insult than anything. My sisters each got several hundred thousand, but, compared to what I got, they decided they were severely gypped. My mother was very much on their side. They tried hard to get me to hand over the spoils of my inheritance and took me to court over it, but, in the end, I won. My grand-mother had left a letter explaining exactly why she had given us these unequal shares in her estate, and the court sided with my grandmother's wishes."

"Good," he said forcibly. "It's unfair to take away some-body's final wishes like that and to have the court decide on a different division of assets."

"Well, as the outcome of that," she said drily, "I might have gotten the house and money, but I lost my sisters and mother."

He looked at her steadily for a long moment and then said, "If that's all it took, you didn't have them to begin with." And, with that note, he leaned over, dropped a kiss on her forehead and walked out.

CHAPTER 7

S HE REACHED HER fingers to her forehead, wondering at the kiss. Was it just to make her feel better? Because any mention of that court case was terrifying. She'd gone through hell and high water, had even wanted to hand it all over to her family, but her lawyer had been totally against it. He'd also been her grandmother's lawyer and understood why her grandmother hadn't wanted the others to have as much.

"You can't do that," her lawyer had said firmly. "These are your grandmother's wishes, and I understand and totally agree with her."

"But my sisters aren't that bad," she'd cried out.

"And they aren't that good either," he'd said in the same tone. "You're the one who came over and visited her all the time. You're the one who spent weekends with her. You're the one who took her around shopping, took her to the doctors. You're the one who looked after her."

"But my sisters would have if they'd known I would get this kind of money," she protested.

"Exactly," he said. "Because they would have done it in order *to get* the money. You didn't know about the money, and you did it anyway." Then he'd handed her that letter from her grandmother explaining her final wishes. That had ended the argument and had brought Camilla to tears many times since. It was a letter full of love, a letter full of joy and caring and gratitude. Camilla had kept that letter. When she had low days and days where she wanted to scream at the world, she took out the letter and read it and held it close to her heart. If nothing else, her grandmother had understood her, had seen how alone in the family she was, how isolated and how so very unlike the rest of her family she was.

Camilla had lost her father when she was fourteen. The memories hurt even today. Her parents had been in a bitter divorce just prior to his death. And that had overshadowed a lot of the loss and grief. Not on her side because she'd been completely overwhelmed with her father's death. She'd even talked to her father about splitting off from her sisters and moving in with him before that. It had been part of the plan from the beginning, but she hadn't told her mother.

With her father's death, it had been more than a loss—it had been, in a way, abandonment, and Camilla knew that was so unfair. How could one feel abandoned when a person died? Her father hadn't wanted to die; her father hadn't committed suicide and left her alone. No, he had died in a car accident coming home late at night. A drunk driver had hit him.

Her mother had crowed about not having to lose out now through asset division in a divorce and probably getting more money from the old bat now too. And to think a lot of her grandmother's disgust and dislike of the family had come from the death of her own son and what had happened in the immediate aftermath. As the arguing had intensified, Camilla had just stopped talking to her mother and her sisters about the subject. Because really, sometimes it was the best thing to do.

So much in life needed to be improved upon, and it was

all Camilla could do to look after herself and to try to keep a bright smile on her face sometimes, especially right after the loss of her father. But even now the mention of her family was enough to make her shudder. Two years ago, following the final resolution of the lawsuit over Grandma's estate, Camilla had been planning to leave town, when her mother and sisters announced they were heading West. As soon as that happened, Camilla determined she would stay. The opposite coast was perfect for her. Okay, Kentucky wasn't quite the East Coast, but it was a long way away from the West Coast. And her family.

As she sat down again in her breakfast nook, looking at the broken French door in front of her, Blyth walked in the kitchen area. "Hey, what happened to your back door? Are you okay?"

Camilla nodded. "Last night somebody threw a rock into the window at the recreation center, and then early, *early* this morning they did the same thing here. No, I don't know that it was the same person. I just don't know why it would be different people."

Blyth frowned as she tried to track that information. And then she nodded. "No, you're right. It doesn't make a whole lot of sense. And it's too darn bad," she said, "but what are you doing about the center? Is the window being fixed?" She could only hope that was the end of the vandalism. How bad it could escalate was guaranteed to keep her awake for many nights to come.

"Yes, Donnie is getting Scott in there today to replace the glass. In the meantime, we have our hands full getting ready for tomorrow."

"And let's not forget the fact," Blyth said, "you must get your own door fixed."

"Blaze has gone to talk to Scott about it."

"Blaze, huh?" Blyth said with a quick grin. "Getting close with him, are you?"

"No, at least not the way you're thinking. But we did eat dinner at Mama Mia's last night. He's a nice man, and I like him," Camilla admitted. She got up, walked toward the big preparation room and said, "Let's get this set up. We've got probably a good six hours' worth of work here."

"You may say that," Blyth said, "but honestly it ends up being a hell of a lot more than six hours."

"I know. So let's get started."

After that, it was hard to imagine how fast the hours went by. By the time they had all of the individual table decorations done, the napkins neatly folded with the silverware wrapped inside, everything ready to lay out on the tables with the respective tablecloths, they started in on the head table. And that in itself was a whole lot more difficult.

"Fresh flowers from the florist, our adorned candles, a couple big centerpieces," Camilla said to Blyth. She looked around. "And where are those missing boxes?"

"We've got two more over here," Blyth said. "But it doesn't look like enough, does it?"

"It has to be. We need to make sure this is all perfect now. Then we can just recreate it on Sunday." And that was what they did.

When Camilla heard an odd noise in the kitchen, she froze, looked over at Blyth, who appeared oblivious. Walking slowly to the kitchen area, she peered around the corner. Instead of somebody throwing more rocks, it was Blaze. He was fitting a new piece of glass into the midsection of her door.

"You found a piece of glass," she cried in delight.

He looked over at her and nodded. "I peeked in on you, but you guys were discussing something to do with flowers and candles," he said. "It was way over my head. I stepped back out to deal with what I knew I could handle."

She chuckled. "You know what? I hate to be sexist, but this is a typical reason why we end up with the roles we do."

"If you want to come and put this glass in the door, be my guest," he said with a big grin.

She shook her head. "Absolutely not, but I will put on coffee." She walked over and started the coffee as he worked. "Scott didn't have a problem giving you some glass?"

"I took it as payment," he said. "He needed a hand to replace the glass at the center, so I went with him to help out, and then I took this piece of glass here so we could fix your door."

"Wow," she said in astonishment. "That's really nice of you. I can pay for the glass, you know?"

"Not necessary," he said. "Seriously. I mean, it's just a bit of glass."

"No," she said. "It's not just a bit of glass. It's much more. It's the thought."

"Sure," he said, "so it's a thought of glass." And then he chuckled. "I'm happy to help." He looked over to see Blyth standing there. He smiled at her. "Hi."

"Hi, I'm Blyth," she said. "So, you're the new man in her life."

Camilla stiffened and gasped out loud.

Blyth sent her a sidelong look before addressing Blaze. "You know how many dates I've tried to set her up on, and yet she keeps refusing? And here, all of a sudden, you arrive in town and take her out to an Italian restaurant. Makes my efforts look really shitty."

"How did you know about Mama Mia's? Besides you just suggested the wrong guys or the wrong timing," Blaze said with a chuckle. "Do you always embarrass her like this?"

"Absolutely. I have spies to keep me informed to maximize the embarrassment," Blyth said with a grin. "She needs to relax more."

"If you say so," Camilla said. "Honestly your suggestions have been terrible."

"Hardly," Blyth said, "these are good guys."

"Sure," Camilla said, "but they're your friends. They're not my friends."

"They could be," Blyth said. "Just open yourself up to the possibility."

Camilla caught Blaze's grin and rolled her eyes at him. "Whatever," she said. "Anyway, thank you, Blaze, very much for thinking about this, and I'm delighted to hear that you guys fixed the center's window as well."

"We did that this morning first thing, then we had to go back and see if we could find some glass for this," he said, "and everything he had precut was too thick. We had to find something in the back. We wanted tempered glass, but we couldn't find that, so until you're ready to replace the whole thing, we'll just go with this."

"Tempered?"

"Stronger, used for windows, so, if people fall against them, they don't fall out."

"Oh," she said, frowning. "In that case, maybe I need to replace the door."

"Not for a while," he said. "Not unless you need to. This will be fine for years."

She sighed happily. "Well, that is good news, indeed. Okay, and coffee is almost done whenever you're ready."

"Why don't we try to get our stuff finished too," Blyth said, "and then I can leave for the day."

"Absolutely."

The two women hurried back into the room, leaving Blaze to work on the door on his own.

HE SMILED AS they laughed. It was such a female move. Most guys he knew would ask if he needed help, but most women he knew wouldn't have thought that as they had no idea what he was doing. That was why he'd stayed to help Scott, because keeping glass centered where it needed to go while fitting it into the frame could be awkward. Of course, they'd used suction cups, but the center's window pane in particular had to be done on a ladder, and it was much better if one man was inside and one was outside.

Blaze figured he'd be able to do this one on his own, but it was proving to be a bit of a challenge. He opened the door and straddled it, using suction cups on either side to line up the new pane. Finally he got it to slide into the top of the frame, and he raised the glass panel ever-so-slightly to get the bottom of the frame tucked under the bottom edge of the glass. Adjusting it and locking it in and all together was the next step.

As he worked, he could hear the two women, not too far away, sorting through the last of their decorations. He couldn't imagine spending days making things like they were, folding fancy napkin shapes. That was so far away from his realm of what he considered normal work. But still, to each their own. Once he was done with his glass pane repair, he stepped back and smiled.

Hearing something, he looked up to see Camilla walking toward him, her face paler than normal. She held out her cell phone so he could see the text. It read **Leave him alone.**

He looked at it, frowned and said, "Do you know that person, that number?"

She shook her head. "No."

"Somebody really has it in for one of us," he said, straightening up. He wrote down the number. "We need to tell the sheriff. He should be able to track that number."

Still pale, she phoned the sheriff and told him what she had just received. When she hung up, she said, "He said he'll check into it."

"Good," Blaze said. "Chances are it'll be a prepaid phone and already ditched."

"So, untraceable then?"

"Yep, disposable all the way," he said cheerfully.

She stared at him, her hands on her hips. "Why aren't you worried about this?"

He mimicked her pose and said, "It's not that I'm *not* worried, but I'm not going to worry about it. Something is going on. We'll take precautions, and this asshole will show his hand at some point."

"Okay, so a couple messages and a couple rocks are not that much to be worried about?" she asked.

"Wrong," he said. "It's a lot to be worried about. Particularly the speed between events."

"What are you talking about?" she asked.

"A rock late last night, a rock early this morning, followed by an email, and now a phone text. So somebody has done a lot of homework or knows you very well and has sent all this very quickly. It's been, what? Three, four hours since you received that first message?" He checked his watch. "No,

I guess it's been more like eight hours since you received that email this morning. And that came in about an hour after the rock, and the rock early this morning was on the heels of last night's rock. So I suspect you'll hear from them one more time today."

She stared at him, and her jaw dropped.

CHAPTER 8

"**H**OW IS THAT okay?" she cried out. "If I'm to hear from this person again, I'd just as soon he does it right now while you're here."

Blyth appeared by her side and nodded, a grim look on her face.

"I would too," he said. He turned to look at the glass door he'd just fixed. "This is, at least, back to normal."

She walked over and marveled. "I don't know how you did that so fast, but I really appreciate it."

"Well, it's a fake barrier between you and the outside world. Just remember that."

"Remember what?"

"It's only glass," he said gently. "And it will break again if this person is serious about coming into the house."

Her stomach caved. "Do you think that's what's next?" She was proud of the fact her voice was strong and had not faded away into panic, which was how she actually felt.

"No," he said. "I'm not sure about that. I'm also worried about your Mustang."

"Why my car?"

"Because it's accessible," he said, motioning to the other side of the house. "You haven't put it in the garage. When you're driving around town, you leave it parked outside too, with the top down, and all kinds of things could happen to it."

"I never thought of that." She gave a hard shake of her head. "I don't want to think about it," she said firmly. "You could get crazy paranoid if you start down that road."

Again Blyth nodded, content to listen in on their conversation.

"Absolutely you can," he said. "For the moment, this guy isn't dangerous, but he's escalated very, very quickly."

"And I was thinking he had de-escalated," she said, "because he went from rocks to sending text messages."

"He went from rocks to stalking," he said. "I get that a rock through the window seems more violent than sending you a text message, but the text message says he knows you. Otherwise, how did he get your number?"

She gripped her phone hard as she considered his words. "I hadn't even thought that through."

"And how did he get your email?"

"That's easy," Blyth said. "It's the one from the website. Anybody with her card or anybody who knows her name could get that email address."

"What about the phone number?"

She looked at her cell phone and nodded. "It's my business line."

"Okay, so that makes it even easier for somebody to get a hold of you," he said. "The question now is, what'll he do next?"

"I'm not going to think about that either," Camilla said, "otherwise I'll never sleep tonight." She spun on her heel and headed back to the room she'd come from.

Blyth gave him a hard look and said, "You're not leaving her alone to her own devices, are you?" Without giving him a chance to answer, she went after Camilla.

He cleaned up his hands from the repairs and thought about it. So far, it had been easily accessible information. The question was, What did this guy want? Because motivation in something like this was everything. If her stalker was trying to make her life difficult, why now? The only thing Blaze could think of was his sudden arrival in town. He hadn't let anybody know he was coming ahead of time, so he found it hard to believe these recent harassing events had anything to do with him.

Unless it was more about Camilla's interest in him. If that was the case, it would likely be a suitor who she had either ignored or had broken up with, but who had expectations of getting back together again with her. He frowned and pondered that. And then he walked over to the big room and, standing in the doorway, asked, "Do you have any ex-boyfriends or anybody you were dating before I arrived on the scene?"

Blyth snorted. "Nope. I've been trying to get her to date for a long time."

Camilla hesitated, turned to look at him and said, "My last boyfriend and I broke up a few years back."

"Why did you break up?"

Her face turned mutinous.

He crossed his arms over his chest and leaned against the doorjamb.

"Point of view issue." She glared at him. "I don't have to tell you everything."

"No, but any secret you keep right now," he said, "could be the last secret you keep."

She jumped to her feet and said, "You're just trying to scare me."

"Good," Blyth said in a hard voice. "He's trying to keep

you safe. Remember that."

Camilla delicately brushed the hair off her forehead as she visibly calmed herself. "Money. We broke up over money."

"That he had none, or that you had some?"

"Isn't that the same thing?" she asked, puzzled.

"No," he said. "It's all about motivation. It's all about perception. Did you have too much, or did he have too little?"

Blyth stepped in again. "He had too little, and he saw her as a chance to gain much more."

He glanced around the room while Camilla continued to glare at him. "How much longer do you need in here?"

"We're almost done," Blyth said.

"Good," he said. "I need to run back into town, return some of these tools to Scott. What do you want me to pick up for dinner?"

Camilla's mouth opened, hung there a second, then snapped shut. "You don't have to pick up anything," she assured him. "I'm sure I have groceries."

"I'm sure you do," he said lazily. "But not enough for two."

She narrowed her gaze at him. "You aren't staying."

"No," he said helpfully. "I'm going into town, remember?"

This time she crossed her arms over chest to add to her frown directed at him. "I have enough dinner for tonight, thank you."

He snorted. "There isn't enough food in this house to feed a bird. And you eat definitely more than a bird."

She could feel the telltale flush rising up her neck. "That's not very nice of you."

He rolled his eyes. "Okay, if you're not choosing, I will. Blyth, it was nice meeting you. Good luck getting the rest of that stuff finished." He gave a wave, and he disappeared out the kitchen door.

Blyth chuckled. "I can see why you didn't like any of my suggestions."

"What are you talking about?" Camilla asked crossly.

"My friends are younger. Less hard, more easygoing," she said. "I didn't realize somebody like him was around."

"He's very easy to get along with. I don't understand."

Blyth chuckled. "Never mind," she said. "Let's hurry up and get this done. I want to go home."

With that, the two women galvanized into action and very quickly finished what they needed. With everything packed away in boxes for the morning transport to the center, Camilla looked around at the neat and tidy room once again and said, "Boy, am I glad that job is done."

"Right?" Blyth said. "Just think about it. You've got the whole evening off."

"I don't know about that. I'm always worried about things to be done tomorrow. I've got this big to-do list still to sort out, bills to pay, invoices to send."

"I hope you at least got some of the money up front for this wedding weekend," Blyth said. "We know perfectly well how ugly things turn if there's a problem at the rehearsal or the reception, and you're looking for money afterward."

"But nobody wants to pay until afterward. They want their wedding hoopla first."

"Did you not get a deposit?" Blyth asked in an ominous tone.

"Of course I did," she said. "I got fifty percent down." From Blyth's surprised look on her face, Camilla nodded. "I might be too easygoing many times," she said, "but weddings are the one thing that make me really nervous. And, in this case, we have at least half."

"I think we should start advertising 'Weddings must be prepaid on the assumption that something will go wrong,'" Blyth said.

"Maybe. We'll see how this one goes. Hopefully it'll go off with flying colors."

Blyth left soon after, leaving Camilla to wander the big house on her own. "Grandma, how did you stand it all this time when you were alone? Didn't you miss people?"

She could almost hear her grandmother's laughing voice calling down from above, saying, "I had lots of people in my life, even right up to the end. They were usually here when I called."

That, of course, was one of the problems—Camilla didn't have anybody to call. On that note, her phone rang. She glanced down at it, half expecting it to be Blaze. Instead it was her eldest sister. She groaned. "Hello, Char, what's up?"

"I told you to stop calling me that," her sister Charlotte said. "You know I hate it."

"Whatever. I've been calling you that since you were little. It never mattered until you got married."

"It's hardly dignified, is it?"

"Maybe not. Did you have a reason for calling?"

"Yes, you've really upset Mother."

At that, Camilla sat down hard on the closest chair. "What have I supposedly done?" she asked. "I haven't done anything."

"Well, apparently you're really close with that boy," Char said.

"What boy?"

"Enid's son. You know, any other man in that village would be fine, but that one is an insult."

"It's hardly an insult," Camilla said in exasperation. "He's not a boy. He's a man. Enid is no longer around, unfortunately for her and her family, and Mom didn't even know this 'boy.'"

"Everybody's talking about you," Char said crossly. "Isn't it bad enough you create enough gossip without this, and now you'll be all over the newspapers again?"

"What do you mean by *again*?" Camilla asked in an ominous voice. "The only press I've had is from all the events I've been hosting. Don't go making up stories where there aren't any," she warned her sister.

"*Humph*," her sister said. "You better make it up to Mom."

"And why is that?" Camilla asked sadly. "She's always got something in her bonnet. You know that."

"Only because you put it there," Char said. "Make Mom feel better. You know she's hell on wheels when she's upset." With that, her sister hung up.

Of course that was the real reason why Char had called. Because her mother was making life difficult for her sister. Not because of anything that concerned Camilla. Only for Char to get her mother off her back.

Camilla pocketed her phone and decided to go for a bit of a walk to clear out the cobwebs in her brain, just to change the air around her for a few minutes. She walked out the kitchen door, marveling at how quickly that glass had been fixed, and headed toward the gardens. There were big lilac bushes and a fence that held all kinds of crawling vines she thought were honeysuckles, and she wasn't sure what the other one was, but it had beautiful flowers with great big long stamens. They were purple with stripes.

"Passionflowers," she cried out. "That's what they are." She stopped to sniff and admire them, taking her time as she strolled along the bounty Mother Nature had gifted her. "You guys are supremely gorgeous," she said with a big smile. She had a large piece of property, just about an acre. Any more and she'd have a hard time keeping up with it. As it was, she had to hire somebody to come in and mow the lawn.

As she looked off to the side, she caught a rustle of movement in the nearby bushes. She froze, not sure what that darkness was. It was a shadow. She waited at the edge of the fence and saw what looked like a dog creeping along the fence line. She frowned nervously. Blaze might like dogs, but she, on the other hand, was definitely a little less comfortable around them. But maybe this was the one Blaze was looking for.

In a faint voice she called out, "Here, puppy, puppy." She knew she sounded stupid and foolish, but if this dog was the one he was looking for, she didn't want the shepherd to go missing again. The shepherd stopped, took one look at her and then bolted across the road. She shook her head, raised both palms. "Great," she said. "Now he'll think I scared you away." Her phone rang.

"I'm leaving town now. Do you want me to pick anything up?"

"Dog food," she said. "I just saw a shepherd come across my fence line and race away to the road."

"Interesting," Blaze said, "but we don't need dog food. I have it in the truck already. I'll be there in a few minutes." And he hung up.

She frowned at her phone. "I didn't say you can come back, you know?" But, by mentioning the shepherd, she had more or less invited Blaze to return and take a look. She sighed and headed back toward the house. She thought she heard a vehicle come up the road, expecting it to be Blaze, but it stopped and didn't turn into the driveway. Neither did it go past her driveway.

Suddenly wary, she dashed to the side of the house and peered around the corner, looking at the road, but she couldn't see anyone. She looked around the yard and saw a long hedge she could hide behind. If she could get a picture of the vehicle or someone, at least it would give the sheriff something to go on.

With that thought uppermost in her mind, she raced for the cedars. When she got to the corner, she peered around the side to see a small car—old, gray, a make and model she couldn't identify—sitting in front of her. And it had no rear license plate. She didn't recall seeing this vehicle before. She took a picture, didn't see any driver inside. She crept toward the vehicle but still saw no one.

She turned to study her house behind her. Had the guy crept up the driveway or crept up the inside of the cedars? That would be way too funny, only she wasn't laughing. And then she heard a sound on the other side of the road. She turned to see a tall skinny figure approaching the car at top speed, trying to escape before getting caught.

As she stood here, she heard the powerful engine of a big truck coming up the road. Relief flooded through her. But then the old gray vehicle in front of her took off, spitting gravel at her. Instead of pulling into her driveway, Blaze took off after it. She grinned. "That serves you right for doing whatever the hell you're doing out there," she muttered.

Of course, he might have been doing nothing. He might have been completely innocent, and maybe he was looking to help the shepherd he'd seen run across the road. Then she had a horrible thought. Maybe he had hit the dog, was searching for it. She dashed across the road to see if anything was there. The last thing she wanted was to put the animal to sleep because some guy had hit him, and the shepherd couldn't recover from his injuries.

If it was injured, it would need help regardless, and she wanted to make sure she gave it. She had money, and she'd save an animal before she'd put it to sleep if she could. She might not be very animal-minded, but that didn't mean she didn't have a soft spot for them. She made her way carefully down the ditch. "Hello," she cried out, "are you okay, honey?"

She didn't hear a sound. She stepped in a few feet, looking around, but she couldn't see any sign of blood, and no dog lay injured in front of her. Now she felt foolish, thinking that the dog would have either taken off a lot faster and got a lot farther away if it could still move. And, if it was injured, she was beyond foolish to approach it. Chances were she would be in more danger than anything. She slowly made her way back up to the side of the road and saw Blaze's truck come toward her.

Blaze pulled over and called through the window, "What are you looking for?"

"It occurred to me," she said, "that maybe he hit the shepherd. I didn't know, so I went in there looking."

"Who is he?" Blaze raised his eyebrows at her.

She explained.

"I'll take a look as soon as I park and we eat," he said. "Too bad I didn't get here earlier."

She shook her head. "We can eat afterward. If the dog's injured, we don't want to leave it out here."

"Good enough," he said, and he pulled in and parked up at the front of the house. He was already back to her side before she had a chance to get very far. She marveled at the length of his legs and at his stride that ate up the miles. "I've put our food on the doorstep. Go on in before some critter grabs it and we end up with nothing for dinner."

She nodded and walked up toward the front of the house, but she kept looking back to see if he was having any luck. She picked up the bag of food, noting he'd picked up Chinese from the local restaurant and saw him striding toward her empty-handed.

"No sign of blood," he said, "and, if she's not that badly injured, she'll have gone quite a ways. I'll track her after dinner." She frowned at him, and he just shook his head. "I'll need the dog food and leashes if she's out there. I was planning on going over to the other location anyway. So let's eat up, and then I will go look for her."

HE STEPPED OUT the door, waved goodbye and walked toward his truck.

She called out behind him, "You'll check across the road first?"

"I will," he said, "but I'm moving my truck up the road a bit, just in case somebody is keeping an eye on your property. I want to make sure my truck isn't around for them to see."

He could hear the worry in her voice as she asked, "You really think that's likely?"

"Let's not take the chance, shall we?" He climbed up into the truck, reversed and pulled out onto the road. There was a corner not too far up ahead. He pulled to the side, did a U-turn and parked on the shoulder. There, he got out and, walking down into the ditch so he was less visible as he made his way into the first copse of trees, he walked back until he was almost across from Camilla's house. He knew he had one spot where the shepherd took food, but, if she had another home location here, that would help too. He walked quietly in the late afternoon sun, and, seeing a log up ahead, he sat down and called out for Solo.

He was about a mile, a mile and a half away from where he'd left the food before and hoped she hadn't been hit by any vehicle. He sent out several light whistles, calling for her, using the same tone he always did. "Easy, girl. Come on. Easy, girl. Solo, are you around here? Come say hi."

He'd brought a bag of treats with him, and he gently shook the bag and laid one at the end of the log and then sat down at the far end. And he waited.

He pulled out his phone and went through his emails, sending an update to Badger and to Jager before Blaze put his phone back down again. He glanced to where the treat was and smirked because the treat was gone. Solo—if it was Solo—appeared to be a very quiet dog. And that was worth a lot in keeping her safe. Blaze placed a second treat on the same spot, walked back to the far end where he was basically out of view again and waited. But this time, he leaned forward, and he stayed still, as if looking at his phone and disinterested, but waited and then heard an ever-so-slight crunch beside him. He studied the dark head of the shepherd as it came forward and took the treat off the fallen tree.

"Hello, Solo. How are you doing?"

She disappeared, but he didn't hear any more sounds as if the dog had fully retreated. He stayed where he was and just talked to her in a low voice. "You've had it pretty rough, haven't you, girl? Don't like people anymore? Can't say I blame you. An awful lot of problems come once you bring people into the mix. But you can't just spend the next few years running and trying to feed yourself like this. It's not a good way for you to live."

He stood and leaned forward a bit, trying to look for the dog. He put another treat down and, instead of retreating, he backed away so he was a little more in view. He waited. Obviously she didn't like his new position. And then suddenly, she appeared, snatched up the treat and was gone again.

He smiled as he watched her lope off through the woods. That answered one question. She hadn't been hurt. And it did appear to be the same dog. He didn't try to take a picture of her; he just noted the dark markings and the white on the underside of her tail. Relieved, he walked back to his truck, and, just as he was about to enter, he thought he heard something like a scream or a shriek. Frowning, he hopped into the driver's side and drove up to the front of Camilla's house again. He exited his truck, ran toward her house, opened the front door and called out, "Camilla, you okay?"

She shrieked back at him, "No, no, come here, please."

He raced inside to the room where he'd seen her and Blyth working. Several of the boxes had been ruined. "Did you see who did this?" he demanded.

She raced toward him. Instinctively he opened his arms. She threw herself against his chest and cried, "No, I didn't. After you left, I made myself a cup of tea and thought, *Well, I'll just sit here in the kitchen and work on my list.* And I was probably in there for maybe twenty minutes, maybe longer. I don't know. Then I walked in here to check something and realized these boxes were destroyed."

Over her head and holding her close, he tried to assess the damage. "Are things ruined inside the boxes?" he asked cautiously. "Have they undone all your day's work?"

"I don't know," she whispered. She grabbed his shirt with her hands and fisted the material in her fingers. "I didn't see him," she said, leaning back to look up at Blaze. "How is that possible? That means he was in the house when I was in the kitchen."

His gaze went around the room. "You have patio doors here. Are they unlocked?"

"I always keep them locked," she said.

"Let's take a close look," he said gently. "It's quite possible the intruder came in this way and left this way."

She shook her head. "They might have left this way," she said, "but these doors are always locked."

"You were working here all day. What's the chance Blyth opened the doors for fresh air?"

She shook her head and then stopped. "I don't know," she said. "I didn't think to check."

"Well, let's see." He led her to the glass doors, and, sure enough, they were unlocked.

"Well, I didn't unlock them. I always keep them locked."

"Any reason why?"

"I don't use these doors, so I keep them locked."

"But that doesn't mean Blyth didn't unlock them," he said.

She nodded, then called Blyth. "Hey, did you unlock the patio doors while we were working today?"

"What are you talking about?" Blyth asked.

Camilla held out her phone so Blaze could hear the conversation. "In the room where we were working, did you unlock and open those doors today?"

"Sure," Blyth said. "We had them open while we were talking. Remember, about flowers?"

Camilla groaned and closed her eyes. "Right, we did. Damn it."

"It's a good thing," Blaze reminded her.

She shook her head. "Just because we know how this asshole got in doesn't mean I'm happy about it."

"What are you talking about?" Blyth asked, her voice rising in alarm. "What happened?"

"Somebody came in and destroyed the boxes of all our hard work today."

Blyth's gasp filled the room. "Oh my God," she said, "is it all destroyed? We can't get more supplies in time."

"Thanks for that thought," Camilla said morosely. "I'm trying not to think about it, but I have to go through the boxes. I know all the napkins have been untied, and an awful lot of them are on the floor. I just don't know if anything has been destroyed or not."

"If you need me to come back, just let me know."

"Give me a few minutes to take a look," Camilla said. "Blaze is still here. I need to figure this out."

"Okay, but remember. I can come and give you a hand, and we can fix this if stuff doesn't need to be replaced."

"It better not need to be replaced," Camilla said in an ominous tone. "We need all of this fixed tonight, and there's no way to get back into the stores in time."

"I know," Blyth said. "Check it out and then call me back."

With Blaze's help, the two sorted through the boxes. "So, napkins unfolded, ribbons untied and mostly nothing damaged, outside of nuisance value to redo all the manual labor," Blaze said.

She sighed. "And the head table's decorations are over there, and they're still undisturbed."

"Okay, call Blyth back, and I can help you retie all these ribbons, refold these napkins."

"Are you sure?" she asked. "It'll probably take us a couple hours."

"Yes," he said, "I'm sure."

She made the phone call as Blaze laid things back out on the tables, and, after assuring Blyth that she'd call if things ended up being worse than she originally thought, Camilla soon made her way over to help him. "As for these napkins," she said, "they must be folded in a very specific way so that the cutlery, once put inside, sits properly."

He just nodded and said, "Show me."

She did, and the two got to work. It did take another hour. By the time she sat back and looked at it again, she said, "Well, it was just a nuisance, wasn't it?"

"Yes, somebody trying to cause you trouble but nothing serious. Although this could have been, if these were made of crystal or something equally valuable and then destroyed."

"The value was in the ability to replace them at the last moment. Thank you for coming to help."

"Not a problem," he said. "I am quite disturbed that you keep having people—somebody, hopefully just one person— coming around and harassing you. This again, it's nuisance value, but at what point do they get tired of that and move on to something more destructive?"

"Like what?"

"Theft," he said, "or vandalism on a much larger scale. Imagine all your white carpets if the intruder were to come in with cans of red paint and throw it all over your furniture and your carpets and the walls and windows."

She stared at him, wide-eyed. "People do that?"

"I've seen it before," he admitted. "Usually there's a lot of hate involved in something like that. In this case it's just wasting your time, and I don't get that."

She looked around. "It's almost as if somebody wants me to fail with the wedding reception. But this is minor. Although"—then she froze, looked at the boxes, the color wiped out of her skin—"did they take a box?"

He looked around, then picked up the manifest and counted. "Looks like they are all here."

"Good, that's the last thing I need right now." She held her hand to her chest. "I'm getting paranoid."

"You didn't get the security fixed either, did you?"

"It's not damaged," she said. "I just never turned it on last night, and I haven't had it on today."

"So, you don't know if it works. Do you have cameras outside?"

She shook her head. "I don't know where you were coming from, but did you see a vehicle?"

"No," he said, "so whoever it was headed back to town, not away from town. Did you hear a vehicle?"

She shook her head. "I didn't hear anything. Being at the back of the house has both advantages and disadvantages. I'm not sure what we're supposed to do about finding who it was who entered my house."

"Do you have any neighbors?"

She pointed to the left. "Thomas lives there. He's around sometimes but not always. He's a bit of a loner. I don't keep track of him."

"I'll take a drive to his house and see if he saw anybody." As he walked to the kitchen door, he turned to her and said, "I want you to go around and lock all the exterior doors. I'll be back in about ten minutes, okay?" And he headed out.

CHAPTER 9

C AMILLA FELT LIKE she should go with him. And, with that decision, she called out, "Let me come. He doesn't know you."

Blaze frowned, then nodded. "Did you lock the back doors?"

"Give me five minutes," she said, and she locked the doors, grabbed her purse, set the alarms, and met him out front. He'd turned the vehicle around and was waiting for her.

She hopped up into the passenger side of the truck and said, "Thomas is a little odd. I don't know if he would talk to you or not."

"Well, let's go see," he said. They pulled onto the road and shortly turned into Thomas's long driveway.

At the house, they both hopped out, and she rang the doorbell. When the door opened a few minutes later, Thomas glared at her. She gave him a winning smile and said, "Good evening. I just wondered if you happened to see anybody driving down the road or hanging around my place recently?"

His eyebrows pulled together, and he frowned at her. "Recently, as in how recently?"

Blaze stepped in. "Somebody threw a rock through her rear French doors early this morning, about six a.m. And then within the last hour, hour and a half maybe, somebody destroyed property inside Camilla's house."

Thomas looked at Blaze. "Don't I know you?"

Blaze grinned. "Hello, Thomas. I'm Blaze, Enid's son."

Thomas reached out a hand, and they shook. "You're home from overseas service, are you?"

"Permanently, yes," Blaze said.

Thomas nodded. "It's not a life you can keep up forever." He switched his gaze to Camilla. "A vehicle went by not all that long ago. I don't remember much about it, but it had a rattling sound to it."

"Right," she said in frustration. "That won't help much."

Blaze stepped forward again and asked, "Do you have any security cameras here?"

"I do, but they're directed at the driveway, not at the actual road itself," he said.

"Would you mind giving them a quick perusal to see if there's any sign of a vehicle?"

Thomas stepped back and invited them in. He led the way to his little security system hooked up to his iPad. There, he went through the cameras, backtracked the video feed, and they slowly watched. There was nothing, … nothing, … nothing, … and then a gray vehicle pulled up, parked on his side of the driveway right at the fence line, and they could see somebody getting out, all dressed in black, and walking along this fence before they lost sight of him in the camera.

Camilla looked closely but couldn't see any sign of the dog. Then the angle wasn't quite right so she still didn't know if she'd seen Solo or not that morning.

"So he used my place to get to your place," Thomas said,

shaking his head. "What has this world come to?"

"I have no idea," she said, "but this is not cool. That looks like the same person I saw running away from my house after he threw that rock at my French doors."

"I'm not so sure that's a man though," Thomas announced, leaning forward. "The person is pretty long and lean, but I'm not sure we can assume it's a male."

"Good point," Blaze said. "But the vehicle, I guess there's no clearer picture of that?"

As they watched, someone appeared on the right side of the feed, raced over Thomas's fence and out onto the main road. Moments later the vehicle backed into Thomas's driveway and turned around to race in the opposite direction. Thomas froze the feed when they caught a clear shot of the vehicle.

Camilla said, "That's the same vehicle we saw this morning." She looked over at Thomas. "Do you recognize it? Do you know anybody who drives one like that?"

Thomas shook his head. "Nope, I don't, but the sheriff probably will. There's always a criminal element, no matter how small a town. Now that I think about it, maybe it's that lanky teenager caught for breaking and entering not too long ago. A couple years maybe."

Camilla frowned. "That was like five years ago," she said.

"Maybe," Thomas said. "Kind of losing track of time these days."

"Who's this kid?" Blaze asked.

"A kid who got lost along the way. His parents passed away when he was in eleventh grade. He finished school, but he seemed pretty aimless at the time." Thomas rotated his neck, as if trying to lower his stress level. "I know my mother had a fair bit to do with him at the beginning, trying to help him out, but I thought he'd left town."

"Camilla," Blaze said, "check with the sheriff. He might have an update."

"He might," she admitted. "Thomas, any chance you can take a screenshot or share a photo of that car so I can send it to him?"

Thomas nodded. "I can take a couple photos here and email them to you two. Do you want me to send a couple to the sheriff?"

She nodded. "Thanks. I don't know how much value this is, but it's something."

"But what's his motive?" Blaze asked slowly. "There's no reason for him to suddenly, out of the blue, come in and start vandalizing your place. If he's trying to ruin your business, that's one motive. If he's trying to do something else, that's an entirely different motive. But the bigger issue behind this is, Why now? And without a connection to you, Camilla, it makes no sense, … unless he's working with someone … or for someone …"

"That could be anybody," Camilla cried out in frustration. "I've never been targeted in this way before. I really don't like this."

She didn't like Blaze's grin as he flashed it at her. But she understood. She thanked Thomas profusely and then, as they walked out, she said, "Make sure you check your own security system, Thomas, and make sure it's on too. I don't know if this guy is just after me or if he's been planning to move over to you."

"Well, he can try," Thomas said. "You should get yourself a guard dog because, you know, with my dogs, it's pretty hard for anybody to get in without me knowing about it."

She looked over at two black labs sound asleep on dog

beds. "They don't appear to be too bothered by us."

"That's because I already told them who was at the door," he said. Thomas snapped his fingers. Both dogs came alert immediately and walked over to sit beside him.

"They didn't bark when I knocked on the door though."

He shook his head. "They did when we saw you coming up the driveway, but I recognized you in the passenger side of the truck, so I told them to stop."

She reached out a hand toward one of the dogs. He wagged his tail and waited for his owner to give the okay, and, as soon as Thomas did, the dogs came sniffing around, letting both Camilla and Blaze pet them.

"Nice to see well-trained dogs," Blaze said.

"It's the only way to have dogs," Thomas said. "Your father would completely agree with me."

"Absolutely," Blaze said. "My father is a huge advocate of every dog having proper training. Speaking of which, we saw a shepherd I'm trying to rescue. She's skittish but I'm hopeful I can gain her trust. I've come across it a couple of times and I've been leaving her some food in this area, but I wondered if you'd seen her, and if you had any idea how long she's been hanging around."

"I have seen it," Thomas said. "But only in the last month or two. It's starting to look a little run-down and skinny. It won't come close to me though, and it doesn't like the dogs."

"That's too bad," Blaze said. "I was wondering about bringing a couple of my dad's dogs to make it feel better."

"It seems terrified of everything," he said.

They took their leave soon afterward. As they climbed up into the truck, Camilla said, "Are dogs really supposed to be that well-trained?"

"It's a combination of allowing a dog to be off-command and still be a dog and to train him enough that he's not barking unnecessarily or attacking people. So, yes, they were nicely trained dogs."

"Would we have heard the dogs barking as we drove up?"

"Not likely. It's a well-built house, and, if Thomas stopped them fairly quickly, we wouldn't have heard."

She nodded but frowned.

"What's bothering you?"

She shrugged. "I don't know. Just something about that feels creepy."

He chuckled. "That's because somebody broke into your house, so that feels creepy, and maybe it's just an extension of that."

"It's possible," she admitted. "So now what?"

"Now I'll take you home, and you'll have a good night's sleep," he said, "because you have a really big day tomorrow."

"I do at that," she said, "and you ..." As soon as she thought about it, she could feel her stress levels rising. "You're sure that window pane in the rec center is fixed, right?"

"It was this morning," he said. "While we're in the vehicle, do you want to take a quick trip down there?" he asked as they were at the end of her driveway and had to make a decision which direction to turn.

She twisted in her seat. "Would you mind?"

He turned toward town. "Of course not."

"Good," she said. "I'd just sleep better."

"Understandable. What time are they coming to the center tomorrow?"

"Noon. I must have it all ready by eleven. Flowers are being delivered at nine," she said. "I need everything done early as some people try to get here ahead of the wedding party."

"Okay, let's make sure everything's okay at the center."

"Thank you," she said. "I appreciate it." They drove in silence for a few minutes. "How can you get close to that shepherd if it doesn't like people?"

"Partly she doesn't like people because she's scared. She doesn't know who to trust, and her world has been upended," he said, "so I must get her to trust me first."

"So you say," she said. "I just can't imagine a dog wanting to trust anybody."

"Meaning, you don't trust anyone?"

"That's not what I meant," she said, "but maybe it is." She shrugged. "This has unsettled me, and I don't really understand what I'm supposed to do about it."

"What you do about it is find out who's behind it. If this does happen to be somebody in and out of trouble in town, there's got to be a reason why, all of a sudden, he's targeting you. And my money says somebody's paying him to."

"Why would they do that?" she demanded.

"Because it keeps them one step away from the actual criminal activity and gives them a fall guy for the crime, so they aren't held responsible, and it gives them the pleasure of causing you trouble. The question remains, what is this all about?"

"I have no clue," she said. "It makes no sense to me."

BLAZE PULLED INTO the large parking lot outside the rec

center and turned off the engine. "We should've come earlier if you wanted to take a good look around."

"Yeah, this is the time of night I'd expect somebody to cause trouble though."

"Are you expecting to find somebody here?" he asked in surprise. "I figured you just wanted to check and see if they'd already come."

She groaned. "I'm just making sure everything's okay for tomorrow. I can imagine I'll be back bright and early in the morning to make sure again. It'll take several trips to get all the boxes here anyway."

"I can give you a hand," he said. "It's not like I'm leaving your place tonight anyway." He tried to make that come out smoothly so she wouldn't really notice. When she just hopped out and slammed the truck door as he spoke, he wasn't sure she'd even heard him.

But, rounding the front end of his truck, she said, "What are you talking about?"

"Somebody tried to break into your house today with that rock trick, and then somebody *did* enter your house. What makes you think they're done?"

He could see from the look on her face that she had deliberately pushed off that issue. With nightfall coming, the darkness and the looming threat crowded in on her. "Do you really think they will?"

"No way to know," he said. He snagged her arm and tucked it up against him. "Come on. Let's go check it out. Do you have keys?"

"They were supposed to leave it unlocked after the event today."

"Did somebody come in and clean up?"

"Whoever organized the event is responsible for leaving

it clean. But you're right, sometimes we have to clean it first. Particularly for something like a wedding reception. It's amazing how absolutely perfect everything has to be."

"Back to that. You're never doing anything wedding-related again, right?"

She chuckled. "Apparently. At least I'm not planning the wedding," she said. "That would have been much too much."

"So does she have somebody else planning that?"

"Yes, because she wanted a very specific theme, and she's got a particular minister presiding over the ceremony, all that good stuff. So they're getting married in the park, and then they're coming here, and that's when I take over."

"Perfect. Then why did they have the rehearsal here?"

"Because they couldn't at the park?" she said with a shrug of her shoulders. "By the time they get here, it'll be noon, but …"

"Got it," he said, but honestly he didn't. He wasn't somebody who wanted a big wedding, although he could see if his partner was really intent on having a large one how he might bow to her wishes, but it certainly wouldn't be his first choice. "What about you? Will you have a big expensive wedding?"

"I'm eloping," she said succinctly. "It would be hard for me to arrange my own, and yet, it would be almost impossible for somebody else to do it. I would probably meet a couple friends in the park and have maybe a potluck or something." She chuckled. "Or maybe cater a meal at my house. I don't know. I haven't really put any thought into it."

"Good enough," he said as they walked around the building. "Are you satisfied? Can we go home now?"

CHAPTER 10

"**I** WANT TO go all the way around once, and then I want to check out the inside," Camilla stated firmly. Her hand slid off his arm and snuck down to interlock her fingers with his. Holding hands, they walked the entire circumference of the building and then stepped in through the kitchen. She sniffed the air and said, "Well, that's good news. It smells clean enough."

They kept walking through, turning on lights as they went. She frowned when she saw the tables. "These aren't our tables. We have to put these all away before we can set up what we are using."

He said, "Tables are tables, aren't they?"

"No," she said. "The bride was very specific, eight to a table, no more and no less."

These were smaller tables, seating six in a pinch. He shook his head. "Again, better you than me."

She chuckled. "We rent a lot of equipment, and I own a lot at this point. They should be here somewhere." She looked in one of the storerooms and nodded. "The tables we use are right here. So they were dropped off earlier today."

"Good," he said. "Anything else you need to look at?"

"Let's check the bathroom." They did that, came back out and she smiled. "I think we're good to go," she said as they headed to the truck. "I should have driven myself. Then you wouldn't have to come back to my place."

"Like I said before, I'm not leaving you alone tonight. Either you have a spare room where I'll crash, or I'll sleep on the couch. If you won't let me inside," he said, "I'll sleep in my truck."

"It's not that big a deal," she said, unnerved but not sure why. He'd been a huge help, and she hadn't been looking forward to a night alone in that big house. "You can have a spare room."

"So, who would hate you enough to want to hire somebody to ruin your business?"

"I don't know of anybody," she said, "and why must it be somebody trying to ruin my business?"

"Well, whose business is it," he said, "that's affected?"

"Okay, fine," she said, giving him that concession. "There really isn't a competitor in town. Maybe that's an issue, but it's a small town. It's not like I'm making money. I do this mostly because it's fun and to help out my friends."

"Okay, that's good to know. Is there any big company from one of the bigger cities trying to push into this area?"

"It doesn't make sense for them to want to," she said. "With extra traveling, again it's a small area, not too many people like outsiders homing in on the local businesses either," she reminded him.

"So, if it's not somebody out of town trying to destroy your business, why is somebody local trying to destroy your business?"

She laughed at that. "Maybe to shut me down? But, if they're not a competitor, why?"

"Somebody who doesn't like the job you're doing? Did you ever have a dissatisfied customer?"

"Sure," she said, "everybody does. I do my best, but

sometimes, due to circumstances beyond my control …"

"Like what?"

"Mother Nature, for one," she said. "One of the seniors groups wanted an outdoor luncheon catered for their lawn-mowing competition, but it rained. We had tents set up, but the tents weren't meant to handle too much rain, and it poured. So we ended up with great big rivers coming off the tents and ruining a bunch of the food and getting the tablecloths soaked, and of course, everybody outside was soaked too."

"That wouldn't have been much fun," he said. "On the other hand, it would have been quite a chuckle."

"It was a chuckle for anybody who wasn't there. It was the talk of the town afterward. But I can hardly be blamed for that."

"No, but I can see people would be disgruntled."

"That they were," she said. "Other than that, I don't have too many disgruntled clients."

"It just takes one upset customer to want their money back or to see you lose money because of something you did or didn't do for them."

"As far as I know, I did the best job I could in every circumstance, but it doesn't always work out. In Sammy's wedding, she wanted blue flowers. Do you know how hard it is to get blue flowers sometimes? But that was all she would accept, and she wouldn't have just a few. She wanted hundreds. I could get a hundred twenty-five, I think it was, but she wanted two-fifty, so she was quite angry."

"Enough to be really angry?"

"I don't think so," she said. "She asked me to be the godmother of her first child, so I presume she's over it," Camilla joked. "But, at the time, oh my God, it was one of the nastiest scenes I've ever seen."

"And you're still friends with her?"

"Well, I declined the godmother invitation," she said. "So maybe we're not that good friends anymore. But we're cordial. I don't think she still holds me as a monster who ruined her wedding or anything."

"What did you end up doing for the other flowers?"

"White with blue ribbons," she said with a shrug. "It's all we could come up with at the time."

"That seems like a reasonable solution," he said.

She shrugged. "For me, it's easy to toss off the substitution as part of running a business. But, for somebody who had their heart set on all blue flowers, I guess it was traumatic. And honestly, nothing is more traumatic than a wedding day for a bride. I know that sounds silly because it's supposed to be their best day ever, but it's so stressful."

"You're right. It doesn't sound very smart or sensible," he said. "Interesting how it works. Obviously I've heard stories about angry brides, but I've never seen one."

"Not many have," she said. "Sammy had one of those screaming fits which I had to endure with her bridesmaids looking on. Not exactly a fun time."

"You really don't think she'd have anything to do with this?"

Camilla shook her head. "No, I really don't. No reason for her to do this now. This was about three years ago when I first started the business, so what would trigger this issue now?"

"Did she just get divorced, because that could be a trigger."

"No, she's expecting her second child," Camilla said. "And honestly, I think she just wants to forget her behavior.

I know her bridesmaids took her to task for it afterward, but nobody dared say anything to her on the day of."

"That's sounds rough," he said.

"It was." She chuckled. "I do various conventions. I do business meetings. We handle many charity events. Often things go wrong. I order sixty-nine tables, and I get sixty-two. I order, you know, dinner service for fourteen, and I get dinner service for sixteen. You do your best, but you're depending on other companies to do their job as well."

"So, then we're back to shutting you down. If you were to shut down, what would happen?"

"I'd be lost," she said bluntly. "Can't say I really like this turn of questioning. I understand the need for it, but it's not comfortable to think about. Before I inherited everything from my grandmother, I would have probably moved. I wouldn't stay here knowing somebody had done this deliberately. That someone hated me that much, and I wouldn't have known who it was. I'd have constantly looked over my shoulder. But now that I have a home, and I have money, and I don't have to work, I'm not sure I would leave," she said honestly.

"Interesting. I presume everybody in town knows you inherited the house?"

"Yes," she said. "And, as far as leaving, well, I don't even know where I'd go."

"Would your mom want you to move West?"

"I don't know," she said honestly. "Maybe now I'd be welcome. Back then she wanted to get away from the fact I had inherited the house and all the money. And, no, it wasn't all the money. Just more money than the others got."

"Right, and of course she hasn't made any move to ask you to move West, correct?"

"No," she said with a shake of her head. "If anything, she wants me to stay here."

"Well, that knocks out that line of thinking then."

"Exactly." They pulled up in front of Camilla's house, and he parked again. She hopped out, waited for him to get out and then said, "You know that you don't have to stay."

He gave a wave of his hand. "Let's not even go there right now. Did you ever hear back from the sheriff?"

She frowned and shook her head. "And it's too late to contact him now."

"You would think he'd have at least responded to your call."

She nodded. "He's normally very good about that."

"Do you want me to give him a call?"

"You can," she said, "if you think it's something we should do."

As they walked into her house, she stopped, listened and then smiled. "It doesn't sound like anybody's here."

He gave a shallow laugh. "Is that how you check?"

"I did turn the security on, and I did lock the doors." She walked to the couch and sat down. "I'm hungry again," she announced.

"The Chinese is all gone, sorry," he said.

"I'm not all that hungry, just picky," she said, frowning. "I could use a hot cup of coffee though."

"It's almost nine, you know?"

She sighed. "I didn't know. I am tired. I shouldn't eat at this point."

"Unless you're hungry, and it'll wake you up."

"I'll have some yogurt." She got up, opened the fridge, pulled out some yogurt and said, "Instead of coffee, how about a cup of tea?" She put on the kettle and sat down, having several spoons of vanilla yogurt.

"What do you do to unwind?" he asked bluntly. "You look like you're stretched too thin, worrying about tomorrow."

She smiled. "I look that bad, huh?"

He appeared stuck for an answer.

She laughed at him. "It's okay. I'm sorry, but I do like to tease."

"That's fine," he said. "I like to tease back too."

She nodded as she put away the yogurt, looked at the kettle and said, "It's still not boiling. I can't be bothered now. Come on. Let me show you to the spare room, and then I'll have a shower and crash. Tomorrow is another day, and it's starting to look like it'll be a long one."

"I highly suspect these days are always long when wedding-related," he said.

"Yes," she nodded. "But tomorrow … I don't know, it just has a rough feeling about it."

"Because of your intruder?"

"I would hate to think he'd do anything to disrupt the reception. If someone was trying to destroy my business, that would do it."

Upstairs she pointed out the spare bedroom at the end of the hall. "There's a bathroom attached," she said. "I'll see you in the morning." And, with a tired wave, she walked back to her room, stepped inside and closed the double doors behind her. Her room looked normal, and that was a good thing because she didn't think she could handle more stress today. Stripping off her clothes, she headed in for a quick shower and then took her long blond hair, turned it into a braid, got into her nightclothes and climbed into bed. She was out within minutes.

HE HEARD THE water turn on and then stop. He hadn't brought any overnight clothes with him but figured a shower wasn't a bad idea. He'd helped out with the glass repairs and didn't want to see any of that stay on his skin. It was amazing how fine glass dust could be when you were cutting it. He had a quick shower himself, gave his clothes a really good shake out on the balcony in the dark and then crawled into bed. He wondered what the hell was going on here in Camilla's life.

He hadn't contacted his father all day and sent him a text. When his father called him, he asked, "What the hell's going on?"

"I don't know," Blaze said. He related the day's events, adding, "I called the sheriff's number just before we came into the house, but he didn't answer."

"Guess you didn't hear, but the sheriff was struck over the head. He's in the hospital."

Blaze bolted upright. "When did that happen?"

"This morning. You didn't hear about it?"

Blaze frowned, shaking his head. "No, I was back and forth helping Scott with the glass repair at the rec center, and then I was fixing glass here," he said, "so I heard nothing."

"It happened before you fixed the glass," his father said. "He was at the center early, and I guess somebody drove past and saw the sheriff's cruiser with his car door open and him lying on the ground."

"I presume they're opening an investigation? That's usually standard procedure when law enforcement is attacked."

"Absolutely, but there's only one deputy here, Henry Brown," he said, "and I don't know that he's done very much about it. He's just a young kid."

Blaze swore under his breath. "Well, I hope he knows what's going on. Our only communication so far has been with the sheriff, who was here early this morning to check out Camilla's broken glass door. We also contacted him this afternoon and sent multiple emails about the vehicle seen outside her house," he said. "Maybe you recognize it. When we get off this call, I'll send you a picture from that security feed from Thomas."

"If they've got the picture of the vehicle, they should be able to at least track down the owner."

"It's old. It's banged up. It's just a small car, and, from the looks of it, it didn't have any license plate because I came up behind it and didn't see one."

"Interesting. The deputy probably didn't check the sheriff's emails and so probably nobody even knows about them."

"And I stopped by earlier, but nobody was at the station."

"Exactly," his father said. "So, you're staying at her place, are you?"

"Yes, in the spare bedroom," Blaze said drily.

"Too bad," his father said, chuckling. "Not sure how her mom'll handle that though."

"Why?"

"Her mom and your mom had a doozy of a fight, remember?"

"What does that have to do with me? What was the fight about?"

"Me," his father said bluntly. "Lily thought I was making advances toward her, and she wanted Enid to do the right thing and leave me."

Blaze froze and then asked, "Are you serious?"

"Yes," his father said with a weary sigh. "It's the one time Enid and I had a real humdinger of a fight. Because she wanted to know if there was anything to Lily's accusations, and of course, the answer was *absolutely nothing*. I never cheated on your mother. But Lily was of the opinion we were heading that way."

"Were you flirting with her?"

"Maybe. She's a good-looking woman. But since when is flirting leading somebody on? And everybody knew I was a happily married man," he said in disgust. "I think all Lily wanted to do was mess up my marriage."

"Was that the basis of the fight between the two women?" He hated to ask, but a part of him wanted to make sure that, although his dad had said he had never cheated, he hadn't been heading there.

"As far as I can tell it was. Lily said something to Enid about a relationship with me. Enid came home. We had a fight. I told her the truth, and then she got on the blow horn and told Lily what she thought of her, and after that it was this horrible cold war between the two women. When Lily finally moved out West, I thought things would be a hell of a lot better. But I think your mom still held some harsh memories over the entire deal."

"I'll ask you one more time," Blaze said. "Did you ever lead Lily on?"

"Did I flirt with her? Yes," his dad said with more bluster than clarity. "I never kissed her. I never held her hand. I never asked her out. I never in any way suggested more. You know perfectly well I loved your mother."

"I know," Blaze said. "And what I'm hearing is, it sounds like Lily was a little unstable."

"She's looking for a rich husband. She seemed to think I would fit the bill. But she had to get rid of your mother first."

Blaze's breath caught in the back of his throat and stole the air from his chest.

His father gasped too and said, "I don't know why I said that."

"You mean, because Mom died within, what, six months of Lily leaving?"

"I don't even think it was that long," he said. "I think it was just before."

"Which means the same time as—" Blaze said, his tone harsh, raspy. Just the thought of his mother having been murdered had thrown his entire countenance off-center. "I sure hope you were not being serious."

"I have no reason not to be serious about this," his father said. "I just know how much Lily hated your mother. But it never occurred to me anything was out of the ordinary with Enid's accident. Neither did the cops."

"And it *was* an accident, right?"

"Yes," he said. "A horrible car accident. Twisted metal, fire, flames. It was terrible. And, no, it had nothing to do with Lily. Of that I'm sure …"

"And what about a cause?" There was an odd silence on the other end. "Dad, you told me it was a car accident, and I don't remember too many of the details. Something about she just ran off the road, fell asleep or something on her way home from a long trip. Was that it?"

"That's what they said," his father said. "The trouble was, the vehicle was a wreck, and the fire pretty well destroyed everything. There were no brake tracks until the very edge of the road, as if she only saw at the very end the direction she was going and tried to correct it, but it was too late. It was at that hillocks corner, and you know how dangerous that is."

"Yes," Blaze said. "But, just as I know about it, so did Mom. That's the most dangerous corner on the entire stretch. No way she would have taken it lightly."

"I know," his father said. "It didn't occur to me at the time. I believed what the sheriff said."

"And yet, now somebody has just attacked the sheriff."

"Whoa, whoa, calm down," his father said. "Remember this was over two years ago."

"Not *over* two years ago," he said. "I'm pretty damn sure we're right down to the two-year anniversary almost exactly."

"It's two years tomorrow," his father said. "So, yes, it is the anniversary of her death. Another reason why I'm having a rough time. Sitting here with a bottle of wine, thinking about all the years I was married and what I lost in that accident. So I really don't want to contemplate the thought that somebody did that on purpose."

"No," Blaze said. "And I didn't bring it up. The fact that you did though suggests that maybe it's been sitting in your subconscious, and you just weren't ready or able to deal with it up until now."

"I'd feel like I completely betrayed my love if I never looked into her death only to find out years later what really happened. That some killer had gone free for two years while I was wrapped up in my sorrow," he said.

"I wouldn't look at it that way," Blaze said. "But something has happened here that brought something very ugly to the surface. No, we don't know that Mom's accident was anything other than that. Right now we do need to get to the bottom of the attack on the sheriff."

"When you call Henry, you should remember him. He was James's younger brother."

"James moved away a long time ago, didn't he?"

"Yes," his father said. "But Henry took on the deputy role. So he's only twenty-five, twenty-six, and he might be perfectly capable of handling this. I don't know."

"Why don't you contact him, let him know I'm in town if he wants a hand," Blaze said. "I don't want to step on his toes but can easily help out."

"I hear you," his father said, "and I'll call him right now."

"I'll send you the photos of the gray car," Blaze said.

"Okay, done deal," his father said. They hung up.

Blaze took the next moment to send the photos of the car to his father, and then sent a text message. **Maybe forward these on to Henry and see if he has any idea who owns this vehicle. It'll take a local to identify it.**

With that done, his father sent him a text. **Contacted Henry. Got no answer but sent him a text. With any luck, he'll contact you in the morning, so be ready.**

Will do, Blaze replied. And then he turned out the lights and went to sleep.

Something woke him up a couple hours later. He tossed back the covers, opened the door of the bedroom and stepped out into the hallway. He wasn't sure what the hell was going on, and then he checked the double doors of the master bedroom—one was slightly open. He crept down the hall and pushed the door open to find Camilla was no longer there.

CHAPTER 11

C AMILLA CREPT DOWN the stairs. It had been that same howl that woke her up. Followed immediately by that weird knowing of something wrong. She didn't really want to wake Blaze but neither did she really want to be alone downstairs. She figured she'd check out the odd noise first. If it was something serious, she'd send him a text.

She slipped down the first-floor hallway, past the room where she had all the boxes stacked. She was relieved to see that none had been touched. She did a further search and found nothing. Relieved, she gave a small laugh, thankful she hadn't disturbed Blaze. He'd have given her shit for coming down alone in the first place. But she'd have felt stupid for waking him for no reason.

As she headed back down the hall, she heard a sound from the kitchen. *Inside or outside?* She frowned and crept to the entrance to the kitchen to look around. She saw a shadow outside the rear kitchen doors. Her breath caught in the back of her throat. She pulled out her phone and sent Blaze a text, hoping he would wake up. When she didn't hear back from him immediately, she dialed him and, with the phone to her ear, watched as the shadow crept along from door to door. She followed the stranger's progress and then wondered if she should shut down the alarm system so he'd come inside the house. Then she could nab him.

She shut down the alarms and, picking up the fireplace poker, returned to where she'd last seen the intruder. There was no sign of him. With her heart in her throat, she froze, worried he might have gotten in when she hadn't been aware of it.

"Shit, shit, shit." She stared at the double front doors. Chances were he was out there. What should she do about it?

Blaze didn't answer her call or text. He must be a heavy sleeper, or his phone battery was dead. He was staying here impromptu and probably didn't have his charger with him. She slipped her phone into her bathrobe and stepped up against the front door. She put her head against the side, trying to listen. But there was nothing to hear. And then she watched the doorknob turn. She hefted the poker with two hands, stepping behind the door and waiting for it to open.

It pushed toward her silently. She waited, her heart pounding and her throat dry, but that poker was up, ready to smack the hell out of whoever it was trying to destroy her business. There was a slight shift in the shadows as somebody stepped into the hall but was still hidden behind the door. She frowned, worried that he'd see her and that she'd lose the element of surprise. She would get in one good whack, and maybe one good scream would get Blaze down here. And then her intruder stepped back out again. And the front door started to close.

"Oh no you don't," she yelled, and she charged after him. She caught a brief look at his surprised face, and then he bolted. And she bolted after him. She started screaming and yelling at him, brandishing the poker as she raced behind him. She didn't know where she got the speed from except for maybe by her anger. But apparently her intruder had terror driving him. She chased after him down the driveway, across the road and into the woods. There he had the advantage. He bolted and dodged through the trees, and she was in her slippers and pajamas.

An unholy growl erupted from inside the woods followed by more screams—hopefully from her intruder.

"Good," she screamed into the trees. "You get him, Solo."

As she stepped back slightly she caught a glimpse of his car parked down the road at the neighbor's. So it was the same asshole. "You coward," she yelled. "What are you doing, sneaking into my house at night, you asshole?"

There was no answer. From man or canine.

She screamed in frustration until she heard a voice behind her. She spun the poker up in front of her again to see Blaze standing there in knit boxers, barefoot on one side, his prosthetic foot on the other, his hands on his hips, glaring at her.

She glared back.

But it was a little hard to be mad when this gorgeous male stood in front of her. And yet, even from where she stood in the odd light, she could see the scars and dents of a body that had been beaten by life. She walked forward.

"He ran in here," she cried out, using the poker as a pointer. "He was about to come in the front door, and I was waiting for him, and maybe he figured out I was there. Maybe his instincts kicked in. I don't know." Frustration still rode her. "But, all of a sudden, he backed out and started to close the front door, and I yelled and came after him. The trouble is, I couldn't really run in slippers." She stared down at her slippers, now ready for the garbage.

Then she remembered Solo and she smirked. "I think he ran into Solo in the woods. I heard a terrible growling followed by male screams. So looks like she's a better hunter than I am."

Blaze glanced at her, his gaze going from the top of her head, down her camisole top to her shorty bottoms and the flimsy bathrobe that concealed little, then to the great big puppy slippers, and his lips twitched.

She smiled beguilingly up at him. "See?" Now she pointed out the intruder's car. "It wasn't so stupid to run after him. Solo woke me. I came outside, and he ran off into Solo, and now we can go and get his vehicle. That should tell us all kinds of stuff."

"Only if he doesn't get there before us," Blaze snapped. He helped her up to the road and said, "I can't believe it. What the hell were you thinking, coming after him on your own?"

"I would have had you here with me," she snapped, "but you didn't answer your phone, and neither did you respond to my text."

"I came when I heard a noise," he said in exasperation. "When you weren't in your room, and I was coming down the stairs when I got your first text. Then I shut off my ringer, and I sent you a text."

She glared at him, pulled out her phone. "Oh."

He helped her move forward and said, "Let's get to his vehicle."

"Don't you want some clothes on?" she asked, her gaze sweeping him from head to toe.

"No," he said in exasperation. "I'm wearing the same thing as if going swimming. You, on the other hand, are exposed."

"I'm not," she cried, wafting the bathrobe edges in her hands. "I, at least, have a covering on."

"How do you figure?" he asked, his hand under her elbow, leading her toward the gray car.

"Bathrobe," she snapped. "It's a coverup meant to be worn inside the house."

"Not outside in the cool night air." He shot her a disbelieving look, and his lips twitched. "All of which I can see through."

And then she said, "Don't you laugh at me."

"No," he said with a straight face. "But it's better than what I really want to do with you."

"What's that?" she asked suspiciously.

"Turn you over my knee and smack you one," he snapped. "I still can't believe you went after that intruder on your own."

"I wouldn't have had to," she said, "if you'd been there. Remember that part?"

He didn't say a word, but his fingers tightened on her elbow. She pulled out of his grasp and said, "You don't have to pull me or drag me down the street. You should be calling the sheriff."

"He's in the hospital. He was attacked this morning."

She subsided at that. In a small voice she said, "I didn't know that."

"Now that you know, maybe you won't be so hell-bent on going after the intruder alone."

She didn't say anything, just picked up her pace. "Don't you think you should be contacting the deputy?"

"Don't have his direct number. Not getting an answer at the sheriff's office," he said. He motioned at the car. "Since you made this find first, you might as well see if it's unlocked."

She reached for the driver's side and pulled it open. And

then crowed, "It is."

He leaned into the front seat ahead of her, so all she could see was his very well-defined backside in snug black boxers as he dug into the glove box for the insurance and registration. He turned on the flashlight on his cell to read the information. "Rodney Pratt," he said. "Does that name mean anything to you?"

She shook her head. "No."

"I'd sure like to know what his motivation is." He laid the identification on the hood of the car and took photos of them. Those he sent off with an email.

"What are you doing?" she asked, watching him. "You said you didn't have the contact information for the deputy."

"Not his direct line at work or his home number so I sent it to his work email," he said.

FOR ALL BLAZE knew, this asshole was still around, taking note of what they were doing. If it had been Blaze, he certainly would have been watching. He checked for a mounted license plate, but there wasn't any. He took pictures of the vehicle on all four sides, and, finding the keys still inside, he popped them from the ignition and said, "Well, he's not getting these back."

She laughed with delight at that. "So then he'll come to the house to get them."

He slid her a sideways glance. "Why would you think that?"

"If he wants them back, right?"

"He's parked outside your neighbor's house. So why would he come to us?"

She frowned. "I assume," she said slowly, "he's watching us. Or hopefully he's at home nursing some major bite marks from Solo."

"I'd assume that too," he said, "so come on. Let's go back to the house. Nothing else we can do here right now. Besides, you shouldn't be up here like you are." He nudged her gently toward her house. "I'm sure somebody will be here soon enough."

"Says you," she snapped. She glared at the woods on the other side of the road. "The shepherd is in there, you know?"

"Did you see her?" he asked, his tone sharper than he'd intended.

"Not other than I've told you but you should have heard her go after my intruder," she said. "It's like I could feel her watching. Maybe Solo is guarding her new turf."

"Or guarding you," he said quietly looking at her seeing the quiet pleasure on her face at the thought. "And somebody else could have been watching too," he said, "but it could have just as easily been your intruder. Did you get a good look at him?"

"I'm pretty sure it was the guy from before, the same build each time," she said. "I did see his face just now but only briefly. He wore the same black outfit, including the hoodie over his head, but I caught a glimpse of his face. Not enough to be able to draw him or anything," she said, "but I think I'd recognize him next time."

"Well, that's something," he said, "but you didn't know him, right?"

"No," she said, "I didn't. And I do know a lot of people in town, although … something was very familiar about him," she said cautiously. "Now that I think about it, I didn't get a long-enough look to confirm that."

"Where do you think you would have seen him before?" he asked.

"I'm not sure, but it's almost like it might have been somebody I saw at one of my mom's events."

"What events did she have?"

"She was big on anything that gave her publicity," she said, a caustic tone in her voice. "But that's being mean again. If there's ever a button that'll get me going, it's that one."

"You mean, your mother button?" he asked with a chuckle. "We all have a few of those."

"I wonder though," she said. "Just because I might have seen him, it doesn't mean my mother has anything to do with this."

"Of course not," he said. "Why would she?"

"Exactly," she said.

They were almost at the house. She walked inside and said, "And, of course, we left it open. But you knew that."

"I did," he said, "but we weren't in the woods very long, so unless he wasn't alone …"

At that, she spun around and looked at him in horror. "Is that a possibility?"

"Is what a possibility?" he asked.

"That he came with somebody?"

"Well, it's likely," Blaze said, frowning at her. "Of course it is. But, if you only ever saw one man, chances are he's working alone."

She looked slightly mollified but not enough for her satisfaction.

"But we should check the entire house."

"It makes sense to partner up, doesn't it?" she asked. "While we're busy chasing him all over the bloody countryside, the second man just sauntered right in."

Together, with Blaze leading the way, they searched the house, beginning with her big preparation room and onto the rest of the first floor, then upstairs, looking under beds, in closets, behind doors. When they finally got back to the kitchen, he asked, "Satisfied?"

She yawned and nodded. "I feel much better."

"Now reset the alarm," he instructed. She didn't argue; she just did it and then led the way back upstairs. She looked so exhausted.

He said, "You need to buy new slippers now."

"Or maybe they will wash nicely," she said. "I'll try that first. These are my favorites."

"Which is an odd choice for somebody who doesn't like dogs."

"It's not that I don't like dogs," she corrected him. "It's that I've never been around them."

"True enough." He watched as she closed her bedroom door firmly in his face. He chuckled and headed back to his room. "I'll take that as a definite no." And what did he expect? It wasn't like they knew each other.

Something was familiar about her though. And he'd been trying to place it since he'd arrived. But, according to her, they'd never met. They hadn't even crossed paths before, so he wasn't sure what niggled at him. But it was there. Something in the background.

He stretched out on the bed, knowing he'd make a mess if he got under the covers. His foot was black. The prosthetic almost the same color. He got up, walked over and sat on the bathtub edge to wash his foot, removed the sock then wiped his prosthetic down. Finally clean, he headed back to the bedroom, only to see Camilla standing there in her pajamas, frowning at him.

"Did you just have a shower?"

He looked at her in surprise. "I was cleaning up. Remember? I was wandering around out there barefoot."

Her expression cleared.

"Is it a problem if I did?" he asked curiously. He knew people had very strange rules and regulations that seemed normal to them, but he'd come across a couple that were pretty unique, and maybe guests having showers in the middle of the night was a no-no for her.

"No," she said, "I was afraid you were getting up and starting your day."

"It is four o'clock," he said, "so I may not be able to sleep anymore."

"Oh." She took several steps toward the door and said, "I guess that makes sense."

"Would it have mattered if I'd gotten up?" He was still trying to figure this out.

She shrugged. "No, not necessarily. I wanted an early start, but I didn't want this early of a start."

"You can stay in bed," he said. "You've got a long day. You need your sleep."

"Yes," she said, "but it would be strange if I knew you were up and I was trying to sleep. I don't know that I could sleep."

"That's because you'd be afraid you were hearing things. I promise that I'll stay in my room for a few more hours. Go get some more sleep."

She nodded and turned away, then stopped. "The injuries to your abdomen and your back, are they from the same accident that took your foot?"

"Yes." He looked down at his hands and said, "It sidelined me out of the military."

"What happened?"

"I was too close to the blast of an IED." At her confused look, he said, "A bomb. I didn't get caught in the blast, but I got caught in the debris. And it picked me up and tossed me, and I landed on some pretty ugly shit too. So quite a bit of severe muscle damage, etc. But I'm healed now."

"But the number of scars," she said softly, her gaze in the half-light on his abdomen.

She was focused on his massive scar there, where a chunk of muscle was missing, and possibly she could even see that he was missing a rib.

"That must have taken you months to years to heal from."

"Which is why I missed my mother's funeral," he said gently. "But life happens. And I'd like to believe she saw me from above anyway."

At that, Camilla beamed at him. "If there's any way she could, you know she would have. I'm sure she loved you very much."

"She did." He grinned and added, "but then I was an only child."

"Whereas I'm one of three," she said.

"Did you ever get along with your mother?"

"No. Never," she said with a half laugh. "For the longest time, my sisters didn't get along with her either. One of them moved out earlier than the rest of us. She stayed with Grandma for a year ahead of us moving here. And we all had moved here ten years ago."

"Oh," he said suddenly. "Now that mystery becomes clear. Fran?"

She stared at him, her jaw dropping. "Yes, Fran, although she hates that name. She much prefers Francesca."

"Of course, I did know her but, when you said you only moved here ten years ago, I couldn't place why you looked so familiar."

"Francesca and I do look a lot alike," she said. "There's less than two years between us."

"So, she came here and lived with your grandmother, went to school here?"

"She did her senior year here. She needed to get away from where we used to live."

"And where was that?"

"California," she said.

"Why did your sister come ahead of you guys?"

"She got pregnant and had an abortion and came here to get away from it all—especially Mom," Camilla said. "Mom was upset about the abortion, but Mom would have been more horrified if Fran had planned to keep the baby. Mom is all about keeping up appearances."

"Sorry to hear that, for everybody," he said slowly. "It's not an easy decision at any time."

"No. Anyway, here Fran could get a new start, so she came early and lived with my grandmother."

"And yet, apparently that situation didn't work out?"

"Fran was a little wild back then," she said. "She couldn't even tell us who the father was. Not that I'm judging her, mind you, but, when she got here, she wasn't exactly up for changing her ways. So Grandma had her hands full."

"But your grandmother had a very colorful life too, didn't she?"

"Absolutely, but she was fairly circumspect about not causing too many scandals and loving one man at a time.

Fran wasn't so worried about those rules."

"Ah," Blaze said, nodding. "I remember your grand-mother. She had an active social life," he said. Of course his memories of Fran were a whole lot less polite. She'd gone through the basketball team and then headed to the football team. But, in such a small town, she soon ran out of guys.

"Did you ever date her?" Camilla asked. "That would feel a little odd."

"*No*, I *never* dated her," he said assuredly to put her fears to rest.

She frowned at him. "That was very definite."

"If anything, your sister wouldn't hold me in high re-gard."

"And why is that?"

"Because I turned her down," he admitted. "Several times, in fact."

"No, she wouldn't have liked that," Camilla said with an odd smile. "Normally she doesn't take rejection well."

"She didn't," he said. "I was considered a catch back then. My parents were both doing well. We had property, the dog training business. My mother was very successful at showing animals, and I think Fran wanted to be part of that. And tried a couple more times before I ended up losing my temper and telling her flat-out, *No way*. When she asked me why," he winced and said, "I was not very nice about it."

"Oh, my goodness, that was you?" she said, clapping her hands. "My sister used to talk about this arrogant male she was just dying to knock off his feet. She wanted to seduce him, so she could then dump him."

"Yeah, that sounds about right," he said. "She used to taunt me with it all the time. But it wasn't a hardship to avoid her *lures*, as she would put it."

"No, she was all about having what she wanted. So, if she didn't get you and if she really wanted you, then you were the one who got away. I remember her talking about you every once in a while. I remember at one point, she joked she would be there, waiting, when you came back."

"While I was in the navy," he said with a nod. "In the meantime, you moved here, and they subsequently left, so I got the best part of the bargain."

She smiled. "That's a lovely thing to say."

"I like a lot of things about you," he said. "Unfortunately I liked very little about your sister."

"You're not the only one to say that," she said sadly. "Somewhere along the line my sister decided that appearances and wealth were the answer to her happiness. Now she has both, and I don't think she's happy at all."

"No," he said, "neither of those two things bring happiness."

"My mother and Char, my other sister, are just that way too. Thinking money buys them love and joy, solves all their problems."

"Oh my God," Blaze said, "the big feud between my mother and yours?"

She nodded. "Figured it was all about Mom's ego, hating to see Enid's picture all over town."

"Yes, and no. It was more than that."

"More?"

"She wanted Dad, and Dad turned her down."

"Oh my." Camilla's eyes rounded. "Like father, like son. ... Like mother, like daughter."

"Yeah, I understand what you're saying. First, I turned down Fran. Then Dad turned down your mom. Yeah, I can see, from their narrow point of view, how they wouldn't want me dating you."

"Let's make a pact right now to never put our two families together."

"Agreed." *And, if we go the distance, good thing Camilla wants to elope.* He pulled back the covers on his bed, straightened them and then folded them precisely but didn't get in bed with Camilla still standing here.

She watched him in fascination. "Most men I know don't make the bed."

"You don't spend a lot of years in the navy without learning how to keep your bunk made and clean," he joked. "It's a habit still."

"Makes sense."

He crawled in and leaned against the headboard, waiting for her to move. He wasn't sure why she was still here. "Are you going to bed, or are you going downstairs and putting on coffee?" he asked.

She groaned. "Honestly, what I'd really like to do …"

"Yes," he said. "What?"

She shook her head, a flush rolling up her cheeks. "No," she said, "that would be playing with fire."

"What's that?"

She pointed to the other half of the bed. "I've been avoiding my bedroom," she said. "I'm nervous for the first time since I moved in here."

He grabbed the blanket, pulled the corner up so she could get in. "Come on," he said. "Crawl in, and let's get some sleep."

She didn't give him a second chance to invite her. She climbed into the bed, tucked a pillow under her head and said, "Good night."

He laughed, turned out the light and slipped down so he was lying beside her. "Good night," he whispered.

CHAPTER 12

CAMILLA WOKE UP, feeling a heat she didn't recognize. She shifted restlessly and finally opened her eyes. No wonder she was hot. She was curled up against Blaze spoon-style. It didn't take her any time at all to remember the events of the night before.

She lay here, quietly enjoying the snuggle, yet really shouldn't be in his arms. It would give him the wrong impression. But neither did she want to leave. There was just something so very sexy about a man who had been severely injured, picked himself up and was back being who he was all over again. It took an awful lot to knock a good man down. But it took a hell of a lot more for him to stand back up again after a bombing event.

The fact that he was *the one* her sister hated—and Camilla meant *hated*—just made her smile. She could see the attraction because Blaze was very good-looking, and of course, his parents were well-respected in the community. They had money and prestige because of his mom's dog-show wins and his father's dog-training business. And back then, Fran was aiming high in this town. Now, of course, she was back in California with her megawealthy lawyer, living the high life.

Camilla wondered how her sister felt about Blaze at this point. Would she just laugh it off as a childish indiscretion, a crush that had turned nasty because of wanting to go to bed with him? Surely Fran married off well enough that her husband's money would outshadow any Blaze had or would inherit. Camilla just didn't understand why Fran had had so many boyfriends when she'd been a teen. Was it confusing sex for love? Easy to do when young. Was it just a typical rebellious stage? If so, it was one Camilla missed. At one time, Fran said having boyfriends was easy. The trick was getting them to do what you wanted them to do. It was all about power, learning your power as a woman.

Camilla continued to lay here, quiet in Blaze's arms, wondering about that. Was that all her sisters' relationships really were? Kind of made sense when she specifically thought about the ones Fran had had in recent years. They were alliances to her steps up this ladder of life. That wasn't what Camilla wanted at all.

"What are you thinking about so heavily?" Blaze murmured, his warm breath against her ear sliding down her neck. His arm tightened around her, tucking her up closer against him.

They were in a cocoon, isolated, just the two of them against the world. And she knew she had no business being here. It was like an invitation she hadn't really intended to offer, but the fact that she'd stayed while awake said an awful lot more about what she really wanted. "I was thinking about my sister Fran and how relationships to her were all about power."

"Power and control. She was all about being dominant," he murmured. "She called the shots, made the boys fall in love with her so she could dump them. I always wondered what made her so cynical and never did figure it out."

"I think it was the relationship between my parents. My

mother is not a terribly nice lady," she admitted. "And maybe that's why my mother held such hate for your mother."

"Sounds like your family doesn't like mine one bit. How will they handle the fact we're involved?"

She froze and then relaxed. "Are we involved?" she asked hesitantly.

"Well, you're lying in my arms," he said, "in my bed, and you haven't gotten up and left yet. That sounds like we're well on our way to being involved."

Just the way he said it made her chuckle. She could feel his breath again on her cheek as he answered her chuckle with a light one of his own. "So, if we're involved," she said, "just for the record, I'd be involved because I care. Not because of anything to do with my family."

"Ditto," he said, brushing a kiss against her hairline. "And your family really doesn't ever belong in bed with us."

At that, her giggle turned louder. "Oh my," she said. "I can't say I've ever slept with somebody like this, waking up in his arms, and you're basically a stranger."

"Obviously we're not," he said. "No, I mean, apparently your sister was after me back then, so, therefore, we have a history."

"A tenuous history at best," she said, grinning.

He shifted slightly, so she rolled onto her back, and he could look down at her. "Hey, I'll take tenuous. Otherwise I'm totally okay with being practically a stranger."

"You would be," she said. "I'm not into one-night stands."

"First off, it's morning," he said, pointing to the early dawn outside the window. "Second off, nobody said anything about a one-night stand. I'm probably good for at least a couple. And, if you want to talk longer than that, I'm up for it too."

As he said it, his hips nudging hers, she realized he was up for a whole lot more than that. She stroked her hand down his back, gently touching the indents and the scar tissue. "Are you serious? You don't know me very well, and, since you have met me, it's just been nothing but chaos and nastiness."

"And you've held up like a charm," he said. "I admit it'll be a long time before I forget the image of you racing across the driveway and the street into the forest in those puppy slippers and a bathrobe with the fireplace poker in your hand."

She looked up at him, and her heart melted a little at the seriousness in his gaze. "Last night you were all about tearing off a strip of my hide for that."

"And, if you did it again, I'll tear another strip off you too," he admitted. "But there was something very special about seeing you going after your intruder. Foolishly, of course. But so very valiant. Protecting what was your own."

"The thing is," she said, "I wasn't trying to protect the house or any of the valuables in the house. I was really worried about somebody damaging all the work we had done yesterday. I need that stuff today."

He nodded, gently dropped a kiss on her nose. "Speaking of which," he said, "when were you planning on getting up, and when do you have to leave to go deal with that?"

"I'm meeting Blyth at eight at the center." She frowned suddenly, worried what time it was.

He shook his head and said, "It's just six now."

She sighed with relief. "Oh, good. I hate rushed mornings."

"Me too," he said, nudging her nose with his. "How do you feel about slow, relaxing mornings?"

She narrowed her gaze at him. "What have you got in mind?"

The corner of his lips tilted as he leaned in closer to her. He kissed her on her nose, her cheek, and then her bottom lip, gently suckling it into his mouth.

She gasped, and he sealed her mouth with his, capturing her breath before giving it back mixed with his own. She relaxed, sagging deeper into the mattress as he settled down, partially on her and partially on the bed. Her hands, by their own volition, had slid up around his neck, stroking through his hair and down his shoulders. When he lifted his head, breaking their kiss, she just lay here, her eyes partially closed, loving the feeling of being held, of being loved. Her whole body was warm. She was still so relaxed from her couple hours of sleep, and yet, he stirred some slumbering flame from deep inside.

He stroked down her arms, dropping kisses along her collarbone.

"That feels so good," she whispered.

"Doesn't it," he murmured, his tongue licking a spot on her shoulder and then the hollow on her collarbone. She still wore her shorty shorts and her camisole, but that was all she had on. His hand stroked underneath the cami to slide up to cup her breast. She arched into his hand, feeling him gently teasing the hard point. She was small breasted, a bit ashamed in case he'd hoped she was a little more voluptuous. But when he lowered his head and suckled one through her camisole, she arched and cried out.

His voice thick, he muttered, "So beautiful." And did it again.

There was an answering pull deep in her lower belly as he moved from one breast to the other. Her camisole was soaked through, but it added a layer of friction to the puckered nipple. Before she knew it, he had the cami pushed up over the top of her breasts and was even now suckling her breast deep into his mouth. She twisted beneath him, murmuring. He eased a hand down her belly and her thigh, stroking her, calming her. She settled in, both loving the attention he was giving her body and at the same time wanting so much more.

When he slid his fingers down, gently under the elastic band of her bottoms, she lifted her hips willingly. He slowly pulled the flimsy material down her legs, and somehow they got lost in the tangled bedcovers. And then suddenly they were kicked off, and he sat up, straddling her thighs, tugging her camisole up over her head. She covered her breasts as soon as her arms were free. He shook his head gently, grabbed each of her hands and pulled them up behind her head before sliding down to kiss her gently. "No hiding," he whispered. "You're beautiful."

"I'm not very big," she said. "Most men want more."

He stared at her in surprise, looked down at her breasts and smiled. "They're perfect."

Blaze had said it so simply with such honesty that she believed him. And she relaxed. She wiggled underneath him. "Now that I don't have any clothes on," she teased, "you're the one who's overdressed."

She slid her hands down inside the elastic and gently pulled his boxers partly down his buttocks. In the front she lifted the elastic over his erection and said, "Shift your position one way or another."

Suddenly he was freed, and she was flipped with him,

settling down on top of her.

She sighed and he whispered, "Am I too heavy?"

"No," she said and repeated his words back to him. "You're perfect."

He lowered his head this time and kissed her hard, kissed her deep, their tongues dueling in a dance as old as time as she opened her thighs wide, her hands stroking up and down his back, her ankles hooking around his calves, and she slowly rocked her pelvis up and down against his erection.

He lifted his head, gasping. "I know we were planning on making this slow," he said, "but if you keep doing that …"

She lifted her pelvis and ground against him. "This? You might want to remember that, although we're taking it slow, we don't have that much time."

He chuckled and slid down a little lower until the tip of his erection was pressed against the heart of her. And he entered, slowly, just the tip inside her heated folds of skin, and he whispered, "You're so wet, so hot."

"So ready," she said, hooking her arms around his neck, lifting her hips and plunging his shaft in as much as she could.

He cried out and ground his hips, seating himself deep inside. He lay here shuddering and then rose up on his forearms and started to move.

She loved watching his face, the emotions, the joy, the building passion as her fingers stroked and caressed, and she reached up at one point and nipped him in the chest.

He groaned and plunged harder and faster and deeper.

She wrapped her arms tight around his chest and just hung on for the ride. Finally his hand slid between the two of them and, finding the little nub, sent her over first. She cried out, her arms opening wide as she collapsed on the bed, but he came down, following her off the cliff only seconds later. He stayed in position on top of her for a long moment, but his weight was held on his forearms, protecting her even now. She wrapped herself tight around him and whispered, "So good."

He dropped a kiss on her forehead. "Close your eyes and rest. You've got a few minutes. I promise I won't let you oversleep."

And she didn't answer. She just drifted off again.

HE KNEW HE didn't dare let her sleep too long. They hadn't set up anything for coffee or for breakfast, and they would need time for that. She would also want a shower after this. He lay with her tucked up in his arms and held her protectively close. He had meant what he had said about seeing her racing across the driveway in her pajamas. He didn't know too many women who would do that. And, of course, it wasn't the house or her own safety which she was initially worried about; it was everything for the wedding. He had to admire that too.

His phone buzzed. He reached across to the night table, found his cell and checked his message. It was a text from the deputy. He gave Blaze a name that matched the registration in the car and said Rodney Pratt currently had no job, was living not very far from where Camilla lived—of course not in her ritzy subdivision but in a cabin back off the forest. The deputy would head out there today to try to talk to him. Blaze texted a reply. **Good. I'd like to know why he's**

targeting Camilla. I'll be standing watch over her while she is at the center most of the day. Blaze also warned the deputy about the shepherd in this area too. **I'd like to keep that dog alive and pick it up when I can**, he added.

With that done, he sent his father a text, saying he'd be at the center all day helping Camilla with the wedding reception setup and beyond, and then he sent Badger another follow-up text and cc'd Jager on it, making sure they were both in the loop about the shepherd. With that, Blaze tossed his phone atop his jeans on the floor, slid out of bed gently and had a five-minute shower. When he came back out, towel wrapped around his hips, she still snoozed. He bent, kissed her gently awake and whispered, "Sorry, sweetie, but it's time to wake up."

She opened her eyes, a slumberous heat melting toward him, and he could feel his groin tighten again. He shook his head. "As much as I'd love to," he whispered, dropping a kiss on her nose, "you need to get up, have a shower, and then we should eat breakfast and go to the center."

She looked at him in confusion for a moment and then, all of a sudden, reality slammed into her. She bolted upright. "What time is it?" she asked.

"It's ten to seven," he said. "You go shower. I'll put on coffee and get us some breakfast."

She was already scrambling out his bedroom door, down the hall and into her room. He just smiled, got dressed in his same clothes, realizing this was one night he should have brought an overnight bag, and then made up the bed and headed to the kitchen. Everything looked the same, but he couldn't help himself from looking in the room with all the boxes. Everything appeared to be normal.

In the kitchen he put on coffee, started making scrambled eggs and put on toast. When he heard her come out of the shower, he called out, "Breakfast in ten."

By the time she came down, the toast was just coming out of the toaster, and she stopped in the doorway and sniffed the air. "Oh my," she said, "I could get used to this."

He chuckled. "Sit down and eat. You can't do all the work ahead of you running on nerves alone."

"No, but I feel remarkably calm," she said. "Must have been something new in my early morning routine that was good for stress relief."

"We can make arrangements to repeat that every morning if you like."

She flashed him a cheeky grin. "You're good for the soul and my body." Then she picked up a forkful of the eggs and tasted it, her eyes closing, "Oh my," she said, "and you can make this for me anytime."

It didn't take long for them to finish breakfast and to start loading the boxes in his truck. When that was finally done, she said, "I think that's everything," but she was obviously getting frazzled.

He tucked her into his arms and said, "Stop, and let's just think about this. Now you have a list. Let's go over it." She listed off everything in her head. "Now go grab that tablet of yours, and let's check it again." And, once they did, she realized they had everything.

She locked the door, reset the alarm and hopped into her car. She headed down the road, and he followed. His gaze searched for not only the dog but for the intruder. The vehicle was still parked where it had been, but, of course, he had the keys. They were in his pocket, and that was where they would stay until somebody had an explanation for what the hell was going on.

At the rec center, he unloaded the boxes for her, relieved to see Blyth waiting. With the two of them inside, he called out, "I'm going to deal with the shepherd again."

Camilla lifted a hand, and he said, "If you're here alone, lock the door, please. I'll be back in about fifteen minutes."

"Why don't you make that thirty and pick up coffees?" She kissed him and then shut and locked the door.

Chuckling, he got into the truck and headed back out to the same spot across from her place. Now parked, he exited the vehicle and walked over to where he'd sat before. He called to the shepherd. "Hey, Solo girl, I'm here. Every day I'll be coming. This spot and the other spot, so you don't get too used to me in one place, but it's still me, and it's still okay."

He put a treat on the end of the fallen tree and sat here, waiting. When he heard a fine crackle underfoot, he watched out of the corner of his eye. And, sure enough, a dark shepherd, looking a little worse for wear, leaned forward and gobbled up the treat. Then she disappeared. He put another treat down and sat back down a little closer to it this time. She came again. When he put down the third one and sat that much closer, almost an arm's distance away, she didn't approach. He backed up a foot, and she came. He studied her coat, seeing the mats and the dullness of her color. She was also bone-rack skinny.

"You need food, don't you, girl?" At his voice, her ears pricked, and she looked at him. Huge golden eyes stared at him but filled with mistrust and, of course, fear. He sighed. "I'm not here to hurt you, sweetie. I'd just like to take you home, get you cleaned up, get you fed and let you know the world isn't such a horrible place."

Solo responded with a very low growl, hardly loud

enough for Blaze to hear. Alerted now, he listened intently.

"That's not working too well, is it?"

At the new voice, Solo bolted into the underbrush. Blaze turned slowly to see who was most likely Camilla's intruder. Dressed in black pants and a black hoodie, the hood over his head, a tall, skinny male stood in front of Blaze, only this time with a gun.

Blaze studied the gun warily. "You know how to use that thing?"

"Sure I do," he said.

"Did you have it when you broke into Camilla's house earlier this morning?"

The shaky gunman made a startled move, then asked, "How do you know about that?"

"She followed you into the woods with a fireplace poker."

He watched the younger man's jaw drop in surprise. "That would have been a great fight, wouldn't it?" He snickered. "A fire poker against a gun."

"She had Solo on her side so she didn't need a gun."

The man's face darkened and he looked around for the dog. "I'll take care of that canine bitch today too. Damn thing bit me. I ran onto the road on the side where there was more traffic and lost her. But I'm back to pay her back for that one," he said a bite to his tone. "Her and you."

"Are you prepared to pull that trigger?" Blaze asked. "Are you sure you want to do that?"

"Hell yeah. Besides, this will set me on a new career path."

"And what's that?" Blaze asked.

"A hired killer," the kid said.

Inside, Blaze's stomach settled with cold dread. "That's

your goal in life," he asked, "to be a killer?"

"Why not? Think about it. You got to specialize in something. I figure I could be really good at it."

Blaze contemplated that. "So you throw a few rocks through a window and a glass door. You damage some cardboard boxes of wedding decorations, and you enter a house in the middle of the night, and that makes you a stone-cold killer?"

The young man stiffened, and his expression turned to one of rage.

That was what Blaze had been expecting—that same anger that needed an outlet, like throwing rocks through windows and glass doors and destroying stuff. Whatever had gone wrong in this kid's life, it was still wrong. Blaze sighed and said, "Who hired you to do this?"

"None of your business," the kid said.

"Honestly, I think it is," he said. "You came after Camilla, and you come after me here. Surely we get to know who hired you."

"Hell no."

From the other side of the road, only about twenty feet off, a man's voice called out, "Blaze, you here?"

Blaze dove for the kid's feet, but he shrieked and bolted out of the woods. Blaze went in pursuit, and the kid was running as fast as he could. Blaze wasn't used to this type of tread with no pathway, but the kid seemed to know what he was doing and where he was going. The trees were dead thick, and he was suddenly gone. Swearing, Blaze looked around. "Oh, don't get too comfortable," he yelled. "Next time I'll kick your ass."

He made his way back to where the dog had been. Only there was no sign of her. When he came to the clearing where he'd been sitting, he found the deputy, Henry. "You came in the nick of time," Blaze said. He pointed at the woods. "The kid who owns that gray car just pulled a gun on me."

The deputy's gaze widened. "Seriously?"

Blaze frowned, turned around fast, realizing, when the kid had been running, he didn't have the weapon anymore. Spying it, Blaze pointed to the gun in the grass. "That one. He's got sights on being a hired killer. Somebody hired him to do this."

The deputy pulled a bag from his back pocket and picked up the weapon. "I can't believe this. Nothing ever happens in this town."

"That may be," Blaze said, "but something is rotten right now."

"That's Rodney though," Henry said. "He's just one of those … You don't want to say a *loser kid*, but, yeah, a loser kid. He's the kid who, you know, if a group goes to steal a vehicle, he's the one left holding the bag. If they need a fall guy in a store while shoplifting, it's him. Meanwhile they're all outside, laughing at him."

"That may have been," Blaze said, "but he's not a kid anymore. He's got to be twenty-five or twenty-six."

"He might even be older than that. I don't know," Henry said. "I will be sure to round him up though."

"At least, at the moment, he's not armed." He looked around and whistled for the dog. But there was no response.

"I hear you're looking for the shepherd. Is she in here?"

"I've been feeding her on both sides of this green belt," he said. "Sometimes I stop on the other side, and I put down dog food, and then I come here, and I give her treats. The trees in the middle are really thick."

"It's mostly thicket," Henry said absent-mindedly. "It's really a bitch to cross."

"Exactly, and yet, Rodney knew a way through," Blaze said in disgust. He shook his head. "I'll leave the dog for now because she's had enough disruption, and I know she won't come back out again while all this is going on. And I was instructed to pick up coffee and take it back to Blyth and Camilla at the center."

"Right. Lizzie's wedding is today, isn't it?"

"It is, indeed. The reception will probably go until early evening. Still, it makes no sense what this kid is doing," Blaze muttered to himself. "You don't go from throwing a rock through a window to pulling a gun on someone."

"And he escalated very, very quickly," the deputy said. "Don't forget. The sheriff is in the hospital too."

"Right. So Rodney probably did that too," Blaze said as they walked toward the road. "It's not that he escalated, but he was probably being directed to ramp up his actions. Now I have to find out who is behind it."

"You don't think it's just him?"

"No, he made it very clear," Blaze said, "that somebody was behind this. And he was getting paid."

"Wow," Henry said. "You just never know people, do you?"

"No," Blaze said. "In this instance, definitely not." At his vehicle he waved and said, "If you get any more answers, check in with us at the center. I'm on coffee duty now." And with a big grin he headed down the road. But the grin fell away as he contemplated all the ramifications of not having caught that weasel this morning.

CHAPTER 13

C AMILLA WAS SO frantic getting everything set up amid those horrible feelings of being late and that something would still go wrong that she worked like a crazy woman. When she saw Blaze in front of her holding a tray of coffee cups, she almost shrieked.

He raised an eyebrow and said, "I did yell out that I was here."

She stared at the door and back at him. "But I locked it."

"Yeah," he said in a dry tone. "With a heavy jiggle, the lock just seems to fall off."

She groaned. "What's the point of having locks if they don't work?" She brushed the hair off her forehead and called out, "Blyth, coffee is here."

Blyth, her purple hair bobbing, came over. "Good," she said. "I need a shot of caffeine." She took the closest cup from the tray and then boogied back to the corner, where she was setting up flowers on the main table.

"How are you guys doing?" Blaze asked.

"We're almost done," Camilla said, "but there's that horrible feeling—you know?—that we're forgetting something."

He nodded. "Always."

"Did you see the shepherd?"

"I did," he said. "I also saw your intruder."

"What?"

He nodded grimly. "And I talked to the deputy." He looked over at Blyth. "Do you know Rodney Pratt?"

Blyth raised her head and nodded. "Deadbeat drug addict, a dropout of everything."

"He's the one throwing rocks, and he broke into Camilla's house again very early this morning."

Blyth turned to Camilla. "You didn't tell me. What the hell's going on with that guy?"

"Just now he turned a gun on me," Blaze said calmly. "And he said he was hired to do the job."

Camilla froze in place.

Blyth faced Blaze and stared at him. "I would never have thought he would go that far," she said slowly. "Honestly, he's like the kid who didn't quite fit in. I've been at a couple parties where he was at—probably crashed in without an invite—but he was always an odd man out, saying the wrong thing at the wrong time, just a complete misfit. And I know he was into drugs, and he was into, you know, stealing stuff to get more drugs, but I didn't think he would do this."

"No," Blaze said. "But, if you think about it, it's a natural progression. He seems to take pride in the fact he's now going to be a 'stone-cold killer,' as he puts it. A hired hitman."

Blyth shook her head. "What a loser."

"The problem is, we now know who he is," Blaze said, "so his career is about to be cut short."

"You didn't capture him?" Camilla asked. She saw the pained expression brush across his face. "I'm sorry. I shouldn't have asked that."

"No, you should have," he said. "I lost him in that damn thicket. I couldn't figure out where he went, and then the deputy joined me. So he's gone after Rodney, and I came here to make sure he wasn't circling around to come back."

"Why would he return here?" Blyth asked in confusion. "I don't understand what's behind any of this."

"Neither do I," Blaze said. "But we'll make sure nothing else happens." He looked over at Camilla. "You're looking very stressed."

She gave him a bright smile, chuckling. "A little more sleep would have helped," she said. But she loved the wicked grin he gave her.

"Well, it's hardly my fault alone," he said in a teasing voice.

She flushed. "True enough," she said. "Now you can give me a hand finishing this so we're all ready for when the first guest arrives."

She directed him to rearrange the furniture so it was laid out as per the map she had on her iPad. "This is their custom design," she said, "so we must make sure it's exactly as it's meant to be."

"Wow," he said. "I hadn't imagined people arranged weddings and receptions in this much detail."

"Some people are micromanagers," she said, "and some just want it to look pretty, and they don't care what we do. In this case we've got both." It took a good half hour of moving tables and chairs to get it set up with the tablecloths and then all the centerpieces and the place settings and the napkin-wrapped silverware.

"Oh, I left the special place cards in the car," Camilla said, checking her big tote bag. "Let me get those." She ran out to her Mustang and frowned. "Where did I put them, damn it?" She checked the glove box, in the front and back seats. She pinched the bridge of her nose for a long moment, trying to remember where she last saw them when she heard a voice.

She turned around to see Rodney Pratt with the box of special place cards. "These?"

"Yes," she cried out with feigned relief. "I was looking for those." She reached out a hand to grab them, but he pulled them away at the last moment and held them above his head.

He laughed. "Too bad you can't get them then, isn't it?"

"It doesn't really matter. Everybody at the head table knows who they are," she joked. She looked at him and said, "What I really want to know is what the hell you're doing breaking into my house in the middle of the night." She also hoped Blaze had heard their voices. She was speaking decibels louder than normal. When she watched Blaze's head appear in the front window, she realized he knew exactly what was going on. And then he disappeared. Emboldened by knowing she wasn't alone, she said, "We've never had a problem before, so why now?"

"You're after somebody you shouldn't be," he jeered. "And you should know you're not allowed to do that."

Now she was really confused. Casually she leaned against the side of her Mustang, crossed her arms over her chest. "I don't have a clue what you're talking about," she announced. "Is this about me, or is this about Blaze?"

"See? You're not so stupid," he said. "This is about both of you."

"So somebody who loves Blaze, or somebody who hates Blaze?"

He chuckled. "And yet, you don't ask the same question about yourself."

Her stomach sank, and then finally she started to get it.

"Maybe you should tell me who hired you. Or am I supposed to already know?"

"If you understood your family, you would."

And that was the confirmation she needed. "My whole family hates me. My sisters and my mother."

"Bingo," Pratt said with a cackle. "At least one of them. But which one?"

She already knew. She studied his eyes, the glazed-over, bright, almost maniacal look to them, and realized he was high on drugs. "You need help," she said. "Why don't you get some therapy, help yourself get off these drugs?"

"Why would I do that?" he said. "I'm liking life. I like it just fine the way it is."

She shook her head. "You can't possibly. I know your self-esteem is rock bottom. You fear that nobody loves you and that everybody hates you and that they mock and laugh at you behind your back."

The maniacal laughter fled, replaced by this cold darkness that made her shiver. He said, "Do you really think I give a shit what happens to you?"

"No," she said ever-so-quietly. "But do you care for the person who hired you to do this?"

"Probably more than I ever cared about anybody else, yes," he said, "but it's not enough. I'd shoot her just as quickly as I'm going to shoot you."

But he didn't produce a gun. She frowned. "Do you have a gun?"

He smiled and pulled a weapon from his belt.

"Shit," she whispered. "I guess I shouldn't have asked that question, huh?"

"Nope, you shouldn't have," he said. "I wasn't going to pull it out right away, but, as long as you saw me as harmless, your lovely little boyfriend around here wouldn't feel threatened either."

"He already knows you're two steps away from being completely crocked in the head," she snapped.

This time Rodney cocked the gun and pointed it straight at her. "Take it back," he snapped.

"Take what back?" she asked. In fact, she had said lots of things which she probably shouldn't have but wasn't sure which one was bothering him.

"I'm not crazy," he said. "Don't call me crazy."

"No, you're not crazy," she said with a bravado she didn't feel. "You're sane enough to understand what you're doing is wrong, but you haven't necessarily made any sense by throwing a rock or two or coming into my house in the night. And, of course, you ran away and left your gun at the last scene, so I'm not sure what the hell's going on here." In fact, she wondered if it wasn't just the drugs. Or something else completely. Like a complete disassociation from the things he was doing. Maybe he was schizophrenic. She didn't know, and right now she wasn't too worried about a label. "Are you off your medications?"

He stiffened. "I'm not taking them," he roared. "They're not good for me. I don't like them. I don't like how they make me feel."

"Right, because now you feel powerful, right?"

"Damn right I do," he said with a sneer.

"But only as long as you've got a weapon," she said. "Without it, you're nothing."

He stared at her in astonishment. "I'm the one with the weapon. You're the one supposed to be cowering in fear."

In truth, the fear made her belly quake and her toes curl. But, with Blaze sneaking up behind Rodney, she was much less worried about that than the ensuing conflict. "No," she said, "because the gun isn't anything to be afraid of in the right hands."

"Oh, you can bet it's in the right hands," he said, once again with that cold dark character showing through. "I'm definitely the right one."

"No, you're still that foolish little boy inside who was always being mocked for not doing anything right and for saying the wrong things all the time. The misfit child."

The person in front of her shifted again.

She marveled, wondering if he had multiple personalities. She had no clue, but she'd never seen anything like it as he started to cry.

"You shouldn't be so mean to me," he said. "You shouldn't be."

Almost instantly the blank-face persona returned, roaring, "You shouldn't be talking to him. He's just a sniveling little coward."

She blinked at the speed in which the personalities shifted. But she knew this was the dangerous one. "I'm sorry," she said, "I was just thinking about how hard your childhood must have been."

"Doesn't matter how hard it was," he snapped. "It's made me who I am."

She nodded.

He lifted his gun hand higher. "I have a message for you."

"And what's that?" she asked, her gaze on the gun in his hand. She was prepared to drop and crawl to the other side of the vehicle, but Blaze was less than three feet behind Rodney now.

"She says welcome to hell." And he pointed the gun at

her face, cocking the trigger.

Blaze jumped Rodney from behind, the shot firing harmlessly into the air as Blaze knocked Rodney to the ground and pinned him flat. Blaze looked over at Camilla. "Are you okay?"

She nodded. "You got to him in time," she said. She wrapped her arms around her waist and whispered, "It's my sister. My sister Fran put him up to this." She bent down beside Pratt. "Why would Franny want to do this?"

Rodney mumbled something, but she couldn't hear clearly. Blaze lifted his prisoner's head, and she said, "What did you say?"

"It's because of him," the kid answered. "Franny said, if she can't have him, you can't either."

"That makes no sense," Blaze said. "That was ten years ago."

"Franny has a very long memory," Rodney explained, "and is very short on forgiveness. You wouldn't give her what she wanted, so no way you're getting her sister either. And, if she can stick it to her sister at the same time, … even better."

Both statements were almost contradictory. The motivations almost as equally confused as the man in front of her. Camilla stepped back, turned toward Blaze and said, "This is unbelievable. I thought it was because of you."

"And I thought maybe it had to do with you," he said.

And together they said, "But instead it was both of us."

"We need to get him out of here before the wedding party arrives," Camilla said.

She pulled out her phone, but Blaze said, "Hang on. Use my phone and call the deputy."

As soon as she got that call in, she said to Blaze, "We need to move Rodney away from the front of the center.

People will start arriving any time."

Blaze helped Rodney to his feet, and, pinning his wrists against his back, moved him toward the back of the building.

Camilla glanced around, seeing the first of the wedding vehicles come toward them.

"Hurry up and get him out of here," she said. "I want to make sure that nothing—*nothing*—else goes wrong." And she ran back inside. She called to Blyth, "They're here."

"Hurry up, hurry up." Together, the two women went through the last of the boxes, packing up and cleaning up the rest of the garbage, moving it all into the kitchen, then some to the storeroom. Out one of the rear windows, she could see Blaze still holding on to the young man over the railing out back. And that was probably as good as she could get right now. And then came more sounds of laughter and vehicle doors.

She quickly opened up both of the front doors and then disappeared into the back. The best of all organizers were there but not there. While she had to make sure the reception was perfect, she wasn't to be seen doing anything about it. Right now, she'd just stay in the back and make sure things ran smoothly. She stepped out onto the deck and said to Blaze, "They're all here now. Caterers have set up the food and are ready to start at our signal."

"Good. I told the deputy to drive around to the back so he's not seen. I can keep this guy by my truck, away from curious eyes."

Just then a vehicle did come creeping around the corner. And, sure enough, it was Henry. The deputy got out and took one look at the kid and the weapon Blaze had picked up. Henry said, "We need to get him down to the station."

"I'm coming with you," Blaze said. "I want to make sure

he doesn't go anywhere. You don't have a cage in the back."

She watched as the three of them disappeared. And then she turned around and went on with her day. But her heart was lighter, and the tone of her world was so much easier to deal with.

And to say things went off without a hitch wasn't exactly true, but everything was minor. The food was perfect and on time; the speeches were great; the laughter and champagne flowed; and her friend Lizzie glowed. As Camilla stood in the back when the dancing started, she jolted in surprise as arms came around her. She turned to see Blaze, studying the group. He leaned down and whispered in her ear, "So, if we go outside, will you dance with me?"

With a soft giggle, she nodded. He led her out through the back door to the patio, where nobody else could see them, and she slid her arms up around his neck. And together they danced to the music.

"You know it'll get ugly now, right?" she whispered.

He held her close and said, "Only if we let it."

"My sister …"

"She hired somebody to kill you, and she'll say she didn't do anything like that. But the deputy has already found her text messages on Pratt's phone," he said, holding her tight, comforting her. "So, yes, your sister will be charged with murder for hire or attempted murder or whatever and may be brought back here to stand trial. I don't know."

"He never did shoot me though."

"No, he didn't, but he fired and the gun was grabbed. And let's not forget he attacked the sheriff." When the music stopped, he stepped out of her embrace, dropped a kiss on her temple and said, "I'll go visit with the shepherd, get some more food into her. Then I'll come back. You should be done by when?"

She gave him a one-arm shrug. "It'll be hours yet."

"Perfect," he said, and he walked away.

FOR BLAZE, IT had been a long day but a fruitful one. They had caught Camilla's intruder, and the responsible sister in California was being picked up for her part in this murder for hire. He didn't bother telling Camilla that. But they'd already issued a warrant for her arrest, and it would get very ugly and very public. It was pretty hard not to when it was sister pitted against sister.

And it seemed like none of this had anything to do with his mother's accident. This wasn't Lily's doing here with Camilla, not directly anyway, and most likely Lily didn't have her hand in his mother's death either.

Blaze parked his truck where he'd last seen the shepherd and then headed with a bag of treats into the woods. He sat down, the sun dropping lower in the sky behind him. It was a beautiful day, around midafternoon, and his heart felt pretty damn light as he sat here with a dog treat, waiting for the shepherd.

Only about six feet away, he heard a sound and twisted to see her coming his way. "Hi, Solo," he said, his voice gentle. This time he got a bit of a tail wag. She ate the treat and then eyed the bag in his hand. He picked out one and tossed it at her. She caught it midair and gulped it back. "What about dog food? Did you eat the rest of it today?"

She gave a bit of a whine.

He held out a treat in his hand and said, "Come and get it. I haven't hurt you. You've been fine the whole time around me. Come and get it."

Tentatively she walked forward, and then she stopped, frozen.

He had a collar and a leash with him. At her fearful pose, he dropped them onto the ground, then held up the leash and said, "You know what this is. I can't deal with you if I can't get to work with you," he said, "and, for that, we must have trust."

Even though he held onto the leash, she took another step closer, and he tossed her the treat. She gulped it down, and he pulled out another one and held it out for her. This time she came several feet toward him. And he tossed the treat to her and then held out another one. At this point, she reached forward and took it from his hand. He held out another treat with his right hand, while holding out his left, getting her permission to touch her.

She sniffed his fingers and his hand and the treat but nervously accepted it and his touch. Gently he stroked her under her chin, the back of her ears making no sudden movements, just letting her get used to the feel of his hand. She leaned into him ever-so-slightly. Her gaze hesitant, cautious, but there—a glimpse of hope in her eyes, hope that maybe, maybe her life would be better. He pulled out yet another treat and, holding it near him, made her come even closer into his personal space. She came obediently without a problem. He knew she'd had a lot of training. He gently stroked behind her ears and down her head. And, while she ate, he slipped the collar around her neck and clamped it in place.

She froze.

"Solo, sit," and this time he used a firm tone but still gentle.

As if the movement was rusty and unused, she slowly sat down.

He gave her a treat. "Now, Solo, just lie down and relax."

And, without hesitation, she lay down. He gave her yet another treat and then crouched beside her. Gently working his hands up and down her back, giving her some cuddles, some love, at the same time he took this chance to check her over. She was bone-rack thin; her fur was thickly matted and missing that healthy glow, but there was a light in her eyes. She rolled, gave him her belly, and he knew her life would be okay now. He gently took the time to love her, to check her over, to inspect her paws. He saw one pad was cut and bleeding, and she was badly scratched on another. Overall she wasn't looking too bad, just in need of some love and some care. More than that, she would need time to adjust to people, time to adjust to a new life. Although from her earlier actions she'd likely already connected to Camilla. They both just needed to spend time together. He stood, grabbed the leash and said, "Sit."

Although slowly, she moved back into a sitting position, and then, with her at his side, he led her out of the woods and back into the world.

He stood at the edge of the road in the woods—crouching beside her again, putting an arm around her neck and gently hugging her—and said, "It's okay. I've been alone without a family for a while too. So I can help you with that. This is a whole new beginning for both of us."

He led her to his truck and helped her up into the front seat. He drove slowly around to the back of the rec center. There he could see Camilla standing at the porch railing, watching him. She clapped both hands over her mouth when she saw the shepherd at his side.

She waved an exuberant wave, and he said to Solo, "Okay, so it's a new beginning for all three of us." And Solo barked a soft bark, but it was full of hope, full of promise and full of welcome.

EPILOGUE

G EIR SAT DOWN in the boardroom beside Jager and Laszlo. "Well, another success," he said. "I just heard from the grapevine that Blaze has found Solo."

"Not only found Solo," Jager said with a chuckle, "but he also found a woman named Camilla, and apparently we're having almost as much luck with our relationships as Levi and Mason are with their groups."

"Well, I didn't expect to become a matchmaking service," Badger said, walking in. "But, with Kat around, it's hard not to be."

"She does want to see everybody as happy as she is," Geir said, "and that's kudos to you."

"No, it's kudos to all of us," Badger said. "So we're four to the good. Eight more to go. Anybody got any suggestions about who or where to next?"

"I was flipping through these files," Geir said. "The dogs are everywhere, even one up in Canada."

"That will make it a little more difficult getting the right person, someone with a home base already to cut down on expenses," Jager said. "So far we've been lucky with the men having a connection to where the dogs were. Blaze mentioned going back to Kentucky, so, when I saw Solo was from that same area, I figured that was a perfect match. But I don't know any other matches for the remaining K9s on

Commander Cross's list."

Geir shuffled through the files and picked up one. "Tophat. Love that name." The enclosed photo showed a shepherd with lighter coloring, but his neck was all dark. Geir smiled as he looked at it and then tapped it. "Every time I see this dog's name, I think that shepherd has got to be in a circus or something."

"Hardly. Tophat had an aggressive ability that was hard to control," Badger said. "He's the one that worries me. Because chances are he's been put down already."

"I don't know about that," Geir said. "These dogs are survivors. I can't imagine they'll give up now."

"Maybe not give up," Jager said, "but it doesn't mean it's easy for them to adapt. We need the right person for this one."

"Tophat," Badger said, "was somehow shipped with a large group of rescue dogs into Medicine Hat, Alberta."

"Which is miles and miles of wheat fields and not a whole lot else," Geir said. "And just because he was shipped to Medicine Hat, it doesn't mean he's still there."

"That's true enough," Badger said, "but do we know anybody with connections up there?"

"Lucas Creighton does," Geir said. "His sister married a Canadian."

"But let's get real," Jager joked. "Canada is massive. Just because some guy's sister married a Canadian doesn't mean the dog is anywhere close by them."

"True," Badger agreed. "But it also doesn't mean he isn't. We'll get some further intel and try to find out where the dog ended up." He looked over at Geir, who was grinning at them like crazy. "Okay, what do you know that we don't know?"

"Lucas's sister is in Medicine Hat, Alberta," he said.

"See? What did I tell you?" Jager said, rolling his eyes.

"It doesn't mean Lucas wants to go," Laszlo argued, "and it doesn't mean Lucas gives a damn about dogs."

"No, maybe not," Geir said, "but Lucas was search and rescue for years. Whole family is heavily involved in it. I think his brother-in-law trains dogs for search and rescue."

"Wow," Badger said, rubbing his hands together. "It sounds like we have our next success story."

"Is Lucas married?" Jager asked. "Because that will completely change things."

"Was engaged—and to a Canadian, no less," Geir said. "Something blew up between the two of them, and they separated. I know it's been eating at him."

"Oh, interesting," Badger said. "Even more reason for him to go back and settle this. Either to finish things or to get back together with her."

"I don't think getting back together is an option," Geir said, "but one never knows."

This concludes Book 4 of The K9 Files: Blaze.
Read about Lucas: The K9 Files, Book 5

THE K9 FILES: LUCAS (BOOK #5)

The world of dogfighting is an ugly place …

When Tophat, a missing K9 dog, is accidentally sent to Canada as part of a group of rescued dogs looking for adoption, Lucas knows he's the natural pick for this job. Plus he has another reason to be in the country. His sister lives there, and … so does his ex-fiancée.

But when he arrives, Lucas finds Tophat was handed over to a trainer who deals with aggressive dogs. The news isn't good, especially after Lucas arrives at the trainer's property and is thrown into the dark underworld of dogfighting.

Tanya used to share her home with her two best friends, until one was killed in a hit-and-run and the other badly injured. Now living alone in a small apartment, Tanya realizes how much she's lost—including Lucas. Unexpectedly seeing him flips her world once more …

As Lucas digs deeper into Tophat's disappearance, the dogfighting ring rises up to protect their own …

Book 5 is available now!

To find out more visit Dale Mayer's website.

https://geni.us/DMLucasUniversal

Author's Note

Thank you for reading Blaze: The K9 Files, Book 4! If you enjoyed the book, please take a moment and leave a short review.

Dear reader,

I love to hear from readers, and you can contact me at my website: www.dalemayer.com or at my Facebook author page. To be informed of new releases and special offers, sign up for my newsletter or follow me on BookBub. And if you are interested in joining Dale Mayer's Reader Group, here is the Facebook sign up page.
http://geni.us/DaleMayerFBGroup

Cheers,
Dale Mayer

About the Author

Dale Mayer is a *USA Today* best-selling author, best known for her SEALs military romances, her Psychic Visions series, and her Lovely Lethal Garden cozy series. Her contemporary romances are raw and full of passion and emotion (Broken But … Mending, Hathaway House series). Her thrillers will keep you guessing (Kate Morgan, By Death series), and her romantic comedies will keep you giggling (*It's a Dog's Life*, a stand-alone novella; and the Broken Protocols series, starring Charming Marvin, the cat).

Dale honors the stories that come to her—and some of them are crazy, break all the rules and cross multiple genres!

To go with her fiction, she also writes nonfiction in many different fields, with books available on résumé writing, companion gardening, and the US mortgage system. All her books are available in print and ebook format.

Connect with Dale Mayer Online

Dale's Website – www.dalemayer.com
Twitter – @DaleMayer
Facebook Page – geni.us/DaleMayerFBFanPage
Facebook Group – geni.us/DaleMayerFBGroup
BookBub – geni.us/DaleMayerBookbub
Instagram – geni.us/DaleMayerInstagram
Goodreads – geni.us/DaleMayerGoodreads
Newsletter – geni.us/DaleNews

Also by Dale Mayer

Published Adult Books:

The K9 Files
Ethan, Book 1
Pierce, Book 2
Zane, Book 3
Blaze, Book 4
Lucas, Book 5
Parker, Book 6
Carter, Book 7

Lovely Lethal Gardens
Arsenic in the Azaleas, Book 1
Bones in the Begonias, Book 2
Corpse in the Carnations, Book 3
Daggers in the Dahlias, Book 4
Evidence in the Echinacea, Book 5
Footprints in the Ferns, Book 6

Psychic Vision Series
Tuesday's Child
Hide 'n Go Seek
Maddy's Floor
Garden of Sorrow
Knock Knock…
Rare Find

Eyes to the Soul
Now You See Her
Shattered
Into the Abyss
Seeds of Malice
Eye of the Falcon
Itsy-Bitsy Spider
Unmasked
Deep Beneath
Psychic Visions Books 1–3
Psychic Visions Books 4–6
Psychic Visions Books 7–9

By Death Series
Touched by Death
Haunted by Death
Chilled by Death
By Death Books 1–3

Broken Protocols – Romantic Comedy Series
Cat's Meow
Cat's Pajamas
Cat's Cradle
Cat's Claus
Broken Protocols 1-4

Broken and… Mending
Skin
Scars
Scales (of Justice)
Broken but… Mending 1-3

Glory

Genesis
Tori
Celeste
Glory Trilogy

Biker Blues

Morgan: Biker Blues, Volume 1
Cash: Biker Blues, Volume 2

SEALs of Honor

Mason: SEALs of Honor, Book 1
Hawk: SEALs of Honor, Book 2
Dane: SEALs of Honor, Book 3
Swede: SEALs of Honor, Book 4
Shadow: SEALs of Honor, Book 5
Cooper: SEALs of Honor, Book 6
Markus: SEALs of Honor, Book 7
Evan: SEALs of Honor, Book 8
Mason's Wish: SEALs of Honor, Book 9
Chase: SEALs of Honor, Book 10
Brett: SEALs of Honor, Book 11
Devlin: SEALs of Honor, Book 12
Easton: SEALs of Honor, Book 13
Ryder: SEALs of Honor, Book 14
Macklin: SEALs of Honor, Book 15
Corey: SEALs of Honor, Book 16
Warrick: SEALs of Honor, Book 17
Tanner: SEALs of Honor, Book 18
Jackson: SEALs of Honor, Book 19
Kanen: SEALs of Honor, Book 20
Nelson: SEALs of Honor, Book 21

Heroes for Hire, Books 13–15

SEALs of Steel
Badger: SEALs of Steel, Book 1
Erick: SEALs of Steel, Book 2
Cade: SEALs of Steel, Book 3
Talon: SEALs of Steel, Book 4
Laszlo: SEALs of Steel, Book 5
Geir: SEALs of Steel, Book 6
Jager: SEALs of Steel, Book 7
The Final Reveal: SEALs of Steel, Book 8
SEALs of Steel, Books 1–4
SEALs of Steel, Books 5–8
SEALs of Steel, Books 1–8

Collections
Dare to Be You…
Dare to Love…
Dare to be Strong…
RomanceX3

Standalone Novellas
It's a Dog's Life
Riana's Revenge
Second Chances

Published Young Adult Books:

Family Blood Ties Series
Vampire in Denial
Vampire in Distress
Vampire in Design

Vampire in Deceit
Vampire in Defiance
Vampire in Conflict
Vampire in Chaos
Vampire in Crisis
Vampire in Control
Vampire in Charge
Family Blood Ties Set 1–3
Family Blood Ties Set 1–5
Family Blood Ties Set 4–6
Family Blood Ties Set 7–9
Sian's Solution, A Family Blood Ties Series Prequel
    Novelette

Design series
Dangerous Designs
Deadly Designs
Darkest Designs
Design Series Trilogy

Standalone
In Cassie's Corner
Gem Stone (a Gemma Stone Mystery)
Time Thieves

Published Non-Fiction Books:

Career Essentials
Career Essentials: The Résumé
Career Essentials: The Cover Letter
Career Essentials: The Interview
Career Essentials: 3 in 1

www.ingramcontent.com/pod-product-compliance
Lightning Source LLC
Chambersburg PA
CBHW071358100726
47908CB00004B/1035